Mine

Kim Hartfield

MINE

ISBN: 9781702745734

One

The goat teat was softer than I'd expected.

Than I would've expected, rather, because I'd never anticipated having to touch such a thing. If I'd imagined milking an animal, it would've been a cow. Who milked goats? Only weirdo hippies and, apparently, me.

The teat was a boob, basically. Possibly closer to a nipple, but I hadn't studied goat anatomy, so I couldn't say for sure. Either way, this teat looked more like a dick than anything else.

It was hard to shake off the feeling that I was jerking off poor little Harmony. Her goat boob squirted milk into a stainless steel bucket on the floor of a poop-scented barn with bits of hay flying all over the place. Stroke, jizz. Stroke, jizz. Stroke, jizz.

Harmony let out a bleat as I tugged her boob over and over. "Enough with the dramatics," I muttered. "We passed third base a while ago. You should be used to me by now."

I shifted my weight on the mud-encrusted stool. I was getting a cramp in my wrist, and the milk just kept coming. Letting out a sigh, I switched to my left hand. Why had I thought coming here was a good idea, again?

If I had to decide for some bizarre reason that I needed to uproot my comfortable life and dive face-first into a panoply of new experiences, surely I could've chosen something more pleasant. A beach in Thailand, maybe. A safari in Africa. Even turning my life around by training to run a marathon would've been more enjoyable than this.

Stroke, jizz. Stroke, jizz. Stroke, jizz.

"You should consider yourself lucky," I muttered to Harmony. "Tyler wishes I was doing this to him right now."

My long-term boyfriend had stayed back in Omaha while I'd taken off on this journey of self-discovery… or whatever I was doing. It'd been tough to leave him behind, but I knew he'd be there waiting for me when I came back. If nothing else, he was loyal.

I gave the goat one final stroke, which produced no milk. "Is that all? You finished cumming?" I stood up and stretched out my legs, giving her a pat on her furry white back. At least she was the only goat currently at the farm, so I only had to do this once.

Her liquid eyes blinked up at me from beneath her horns as I prepared to release her from her halter. The bucket seemed to have less liquid than it had when Margo showed me how to do this. Harmony must've been feeling less milky today.

The barn door clomped open, and I stood up

straight like a soldier reporting at boot camp. Speak of the devil. Margo strode inside, flicking a piece of hair back from her face and leaving a smudge of dirt behind. If she noticed the way I'd immediately stood to attention, she didn't show it. She ignored me completely until she finished staring into Harmony's pail.

"What is this?" she asked, straightening up with a hard look on her face.

Her features were as rugged and weather-beaten as the clothes she wore. She was older than me - mid-thirties, maybe forty - and couldn't have been more different from me if she'd tried. I'd bet my life savings that she'd never pored over a fashion magazine in her life. I doubted she'd ever worn make-up.

Her style was simple and practical - well-worn jeans and oversized flannel shirts over cowboy boots. Streaks of gray ran through the brown in her low ponytail, and gentle crow's feet had formed by her eyes.

Somehow, the result was attractive. Ever since I'd arrived on her farm a week ago, I kept finding myself staring at her. She was a strong, powerful woman, and that made her completely intimidating.

"It's... um... milk," I said, unsure of what answer she was looking for.

She set the pail down. "I mean, where's the rest of it?" Seeing my confusion, she shook her head. "Never mind. I'll do it myself." She sat on the stool I'd just vacated and took Harmony's goat-teat in both hands.

"I already – "

I stared as a spray of milk jetted out of Harmony, hitting the bucket with a stronger splatter than anything I'd gotten. Margo worked on her for a few long seconds before finally looking up at my hot face.

"Was this how you were doing it, Cherry?" she asked, still milking the goat.

My stare went to her hands. I'd forgotten I was supposed to use both hands, but everything else she was doing looked the same. Didn't it?

The bucket was rapidly filling while I considered the question. Margo had gotten more milk out of Harmony in the past minute than I had in half an hour.

"Not exactly," I finally said.

Turning her gaze back to the teat, she pursed her lips as if suppressing a sigh. I quivered in my low-heeled Gucci boots. I'd splurged on them for this trip, thinking I'd need them when I got here. One look at Margo's beat-up leather ones with the genuine spurs, and I'd known I was wrong.

"You can't leave that amount of milk in a goat," she said harshly. "She needs to be milked – properly – or she'll stop producing, and she'll be in extreme pain. She'll only give milk for ten months after having a kid, and I'm not planning to breed her again. The one I sold was her last one. This milk is limited and it's valuable to this farm. We can't just go to the store and pick up a carton, you understand that?"

"Yes." My response was barely a whisper.

"Come here." Speaking more kindly now that the lecture was over, she gestured with her head for me to crouch beside her. "Look at what I'm doing. Left hand on the teat, thumb and index finger around. Squeeze down. Right hand on the teat, thumb and index finger around. Squeeze down."

I blinked a few times. So I wasn't supposed to stroke it?

"You give it a squeeze. Gentle, but firm." She seemed gentle but firm herself as she showed me how she was doing it. "You're not doing something dirty to the goat. You're milking her."

I coughed. "How did you know how I was doing it?"

"That's what all you city people tend to do. I guess you can't get your minds out of the gutters out there." She let go of Harmony, moving off the stool so I could take it while she crouched next to me. "Give it another try. She's almost milked out."

With my hands shaking slightly, I took the goat's teat again. I had to do it right this time. Every cell in my body wanted nothing more than to please Margo. Impressing her would be even better. I wasn't one of those silly city people - not just one, anyway. I could learn how to milk a goat, and how to do whatever other earthy farm work she was going to have me do over the next three months.

So far, I hadn't been doing too great. I'd failed at planting - the holes I dug were too shallow, then too deep. I'd given her own meat to the barn cats, and I'd pulled up seedlings when I was supposed to be pulling weeds.

But this was different. I could do this - if I believed in myself, I was sure I could.

I took a deep breath, closed my eyes. I was capable. I was confident.

I squeezed the goat's teat and pulled down.

A squirt of milk came out - not as much as Margo had gotten, but more than I'd managed before. I chanced a look over my shoulder at the older woman, her arms crossed as she surveyed me. The expression on her face was difficult to read. Not happiness exactly, but maybe approval.

"Better," she said, giving me a quick pat on the back. "You'll try again tomorrow."

Her boots kicked up bits of hay as she walked past me. The place where she'd touched me burned as if she'd branded me. I gave Harmony one last look, sucking in a deep breath as I let her loose from her halter. She bleated softly as if to say I might be all right after all.

I wasn't so sure about that, but I'd leave her to her opinion. I headed out of the barn and toward to the house. The air smelled better out here - fresh and clean, rather than the mix of manure, animals, animal feed, and wood that was in the barn.

I rounded a corner and the house loomed in front of me, all curved lines and huge windows. Every time I saw it, I was amazed. It looked like it'd grown out of the ground, like it was a plant or a tree rather than a manmade structure.

Margo had told me in one of her rare moments of offering information that the type of house was called an Earthship, an eco-friendly building constructed from used tires packed with dirt and other upcycled materials. Like everything in this place, it was all natural and organic. She'd built it herself over the course of a year, even setting up the solar energy system without outside help. She'd lived in a tent until the house was habitable.

All I'd been able to say during the conversation was, "Wow." I lost my usual wit and my ability to make casual conversation when it came to Margo. Everything she said or did was so far outside my usual frame of reference, I didn't even know where to start.

I wiped a hand across my forehead. It was only late spring, but the day looked like it was going to be humid. Even the grass on either side of the cobblestone path – probably also built by Margo – was packed with dew.

Briefly I wondered if the humidity bothered Margo. Then I laughed at myself for even thinking of the question.

In the past week since I'd arrived here, I'd seen her spend hours transporting seedlings into the soil, swat away swarms of bees, and wade ankle-deep through goat shit. Nothing seemed to bother her in the slightest.

Nothing but a twenty-two-year-old city girl named Cherry.

Two

The day finally over, I lay on the twin bed in the bedroom Margo had allotted me. The room was small and dark, with bare clay walls. Although all the upcycled parts were concealed, I couldn't forget the house was full of old tires and glass bottles. It was surprisingly warm in here, which was good because the plaid blanket she'd given me was old and ratty.

Still, I was lucky. Margo had said she usually had her helpers stay in tents. Only the long-term ones got a room in the Earthship.

The ones like me.

I threw a dirt-encrusted arm over my forehead. Was I even going to make it through three months here? I could leave anytime I wanted. If I was that bad at this, I could give up and go.

It wasn't like I was being paid. I'd come here to learn, to give my limited capabilities in exchange for room and board. Margo had taken me in hopes that I'd be able to help her eventually. But if that wasn't working, if I was taking more than I gave, shouldn't I just go?

I grabbed my phone, hoping I'd have reception today. Being this far into the country, it was a hit-or-miss situation. I'd exchanged a few texts with Tyler, but hadn't managed to get him on the phone yet.

Two bars… no, three! I pressed the button to dial him while I could. He probably wouldn't hear it – at this hour, he'd be at the gym or getting drinks with his friends. Still, if I could hear his voice on the voicemail, it'd be a little taste of home that I sorely needed.

"Hey… Cherry?"

I sat up straight. "Tyler," I breathed. "How are you?"

The deep, familiar tones of his voice resonated through the phone line. "Not bad," he said. "How about you? Farm life treating you good?"

"I don't know." I let out a sigh. "Not really. I can't seem to do anything right."

"Like what?"

Curling into a ball, I gave him a short version of all the many things that had gone wrong, ending with tonight's disaster. "I know how to cook, right? I cook at home all the time. But Margo has a gas stove, and when I went to take the lid off the pot I was using, I set the damn towel on fire!"

"That's not so bad," he said soothingly. "She should understand."

"She doesn't!" I pressed my hand to my face. "She said I'm off cooking duty. Indefinitely."

"Well, that just seems mean. She should understand that everyone makes mistakes."

Tyler sounded offended on my behalf now. "And as for the rest of it, she knew you were a city girl when she agreed to host you. She can't expect you to learn everything within the first week. She needs to cut you some slack."

"She is mean. That's exactly what I've been thinking!" He was actually more forgiving of me than I was myself. "She doesn't seem to understand where I'm coming from at all. Like yeah, I'm new at all of this, but at least I'm interested - at least I'm trying. This woman barely even speaks to me, aside from ordering me around and telling me I'm doing everything wrong."

"She's not friendly?"

"Are you kidding? She's never asked me anything about my life, what brought me here, what I left behind... anything. She doesn't share anything, either. All I know about her is that she knows how to farm - and from the way she acts, she knew how to do everything perfectly from the day she was born. It's straight-up rude."

I didn't know where she was from, whether she'd always lived here, what she did for fun - any of the major things that people shared with each other when they first met. She'd shut down my early attempts at conversation, and I'd stopped trying after a few days.

"Are you sure this is what you want to do?" Tyler sounded even more sympathetic.

I couldn't stand his pity. I'd gotten enough of

that over the past year. I was done with that. Part of the reason I'd come here was simply to avoid that – to have another shot at just being like everyone else.

His concern had been refreshing at first. Now it was getting suffocating, like it had been at home. He'd been so intense about not wanting me to leave. It'd felt like I was escaping him when I'd finally gone.

"Of course it's what I want to do," I snapped.

But he knew me better than that. "You could always come home, you know. Move back in with your mom. Or with me."

My voice went small. "I've been debating it," I admitted. "I feel like if I'm not meant for this life, I might as well give up."

"You'd really come home?"

His excitement made my heart hurt. I wished I could tell him I was serious. In reality, I couldn't give up like that. I wasn't that type of person.

"No," I said. "I'm just frustrated."

"Because I miss you like crazy here," he said. "If you did come back, you'd have your old job back any time you wanted it. Joe keeps talking about how we lost our best car salesperson. Literally every day he says something about how much worse we're doing without you."

I smiled slightly. It was funny, I wouldn't have said I missed him that much. The familiarity, yes

- but him as a person, not really. He got on my nerves as often as not. We'd been together for three years, and at this point I took his presence in my life as a given. He'd stuck with me through a lot.

"I wish I could visit you," he said.

"I'm sorry."

I'd intentionally chosen to travel too far for that to be possible. I'd gone from Omaha to a remote farm in the middle of nowhere, a detour off the route to Boise, Idaho - and roughly an eighteen-hour drive from home. I wanted to be a million miles from every aspect of my former life.

The last thing I wanted was Tyler - or worse, one of my family members - showing up here. This was a time for me to stand on my own. I was here to find the real me, which meant I needed space. Seeing Tyler would only hold me back.

I probably missed my job more than him, actually. Working at the car dealership always kept me on my toes. Every day there were new customers, new challenges to overcome. I'd gotten the job straight out of college, and over the past year, I'd pretty much mastered it. I'd been on track to become one of the top salespeople in the state, and then… things had happened, and I'd realized the work ultimately left me unfulfilled.

"I know you're not going to come back," he said. "You don't have to do this if you're not enjoying it, though. You just wanted to try new things, after…"

"Yeah, I know."

We were both quiet for a moment.

Tyler was the first to speak again. "Maybe you could find another farm to go to if this lady is that mean. You could find somewhere with people you click a little better with. Maybe somewhere that it's not just you and the owner."

I frowned. I hadn't thought of that option. I wouldn't really be giving up if I was still working on a farm. I'd just be finding somewhere that was more suitable for me. I could still learn all the practical, back-to-the-land skills that I'd been craving, the ones that I'd somehow decided would give my life more meaning.

Margo's face drifted through my mind – her glittering gray eyes hard, her full lips pinched in disapproval. Wouldn't it still be a failure if I went somewhere else? If I gave up on this particular farm – on this particular woman?

Some part of me was desperate to win Margo's respect. Whether that was because it seemed impossible with her specifically, or if I just couldn't stand people not liking me in general – I didn't know, and it didn't matter.

I couldn't give up.

"No," I finally said. "I need to do this. Here. With her."

"Are you sure, Cherry?"

"I think I am."

The cell signal was fading, which was okay because I could hear the disappointment in his voice. I'd barely asked him about what was going on with him, but that'd have to wait for another time. After telling him I had to go, we hung up.

I flopped back on the bed, not wanting to get up. The shower I still needed to take could wait another few minutes. Other than that, I had nowhere to go and no one to talk to. Margo was the only one around, and I wasn't about to try breaking through her unfriendliness at a time like this.

A sound came from the other room. A cough - that sounded as clear as if Margo had been right next to me.

The blood drained from my face. She must've heard every word I'd said to Tyler.

THREE

I spent most of the night tossing and turning, worrying about how and when the shit was going to hit the fan. Margo had heard me describe her as mean, rude, and unfriendly. I'd also talked about how I was so frustrated with my experience here that I was seriously considering going somewhere else. I wouldn't have been too happy with me if I were in her shoes.

But when I edged into the kitchen for breakfast, she looked like her usual self. "Morning," she said, handing me a plate of scrambled eggs and toast.

"Good morning." I looked at her cautiously, searching her light gray eyes for hidden animosity. There was none that I could see, and I was good at reading people. That was how I'd become the top salesperson in my company.

"How'd you sleep?" She turned away from me to pour herself a coffee. She hadn't put her hair in its usual ponytail yet, and it fell around her toned shoulders in soft, gray-streaked waves.

That single question was more than she usually asked me. Had she not heard the conversation after all? No, she must've. I poked my fork through some eggs, my chest tight. If she wasn't going to bring it up, maybe I should do it myself. I'd never been one to avoid conflict. Then again, she was more intimidating than anyone else in my life.

"I slept okay," I said slowly. "I'm still getting used to waking up at six." I glanced at the window, where the sun was just barely peeking over the horizon.

I was still getting used to a lot of things here. Even the food was completely different from what I was used to. I normally tried to eat healthy, but ended up grabbing a burger and fries a few times a week… or every day, if I didn't have time to meal prep on the weekends.

Here, everything was organic and local whole foods. Margo had canned and frozen a lot from her farm's last harvest. She bought other stuff in bulk when she went into town, like the huge bags of rice and dried beans. The rest, like the eggs, was given to her by her neighbors. Fresh from the chicken, she'd told me.

"Right," Margo said. "I suppose you wouldn't be used to how things work on a farm. We need to use every minute of daylight. You'll be glad to get up so early once summer hits, though. There's a big difference in how the sun feels shining on you at seven versus at noon. Work all morning, have a big lunch and a long nap, then get back out there to finish things up before dinner." She paused. "That's assuming you'll still be here in the summer."

"I will," I said, trying to sound firm. "Three months, just like we planned."

She took a bite of her eggs. "If you think you'd prefer to leave, you're free to."

My stomach dropped. "Do you want me to?" Was I doing that badly? Or had I offended her that much?

"I didn't say that." She set down her fork. "Look, we may have gotten off on the wrong foot. I've had experiences with volunteers saying they'll come for the summer, then leaving after a week. It's happened more times than I can count."

"Okay…" That could have more to do with her unfriendly attitude than with farm life, if you asked me.

"I don't fault them for that – this life isn't for everyone, and if they're not enjoying it, I have no interest in keeping them here. I'm not a kidnapper or a jail warden. But I got tired of welcoming people and getting to know them, just for them to take off the moment they get bored."

I frowned at her. She was speaking more openly and honestly than ever before, and she wasn't mad at me. She seemed frustrated. Hurt, even.

This super-smart, tough, independent, badass female farmer seemed human.

"I get it," I said slowly. "I wouldn't like that, either."

"I wish people would realize they don't have to commit to the full summer upfront," she said, staring at her plate. "If you've never farmed before, come for a week! See how you like it. But no, it's always a month, two months, three months. Seems like the longer they want to come for, the higher their expectations are, and the less likely they'll make it to the end."

"I plan to make it to the end. It's been a week, and I'm nowhere near ready to leave yet."

She eyed me warily, taking a sip of coffee. "Like I said, don't feel obliged. You should be having fun. You're not getting paid for this."

"Oh, I'm aware." We shared a brief, awkward laugh. "I didn't come here to profit," I went on. "I was making money at home - plenty of it."

"So why did you come?" Her gaze fixed on me harder than ever. "What makes a city girl decide to uproot herself and head into the countryside to do things that - forgive me - she knows absolutely nothing about?"

My heart beat faster. "I was tired of my job," I said carefully. "It wasn't fulfilling me anymore."

"And why not?" she asked, still peering into my eyes as if she'd find the answer there. "What changed?"

I broke her gaze to look down at my plate. Moving my fork through my eggs, I questioned whether I should tell her the full truth. Her voice, her whole attitude, was so commanding -

it made me want to tell her, to not keep secrets.

But that was why I'd come here – so that it could be a secret.

"Nothing changed." I shoved eggs into my mouth. "That was the problem. I'd just about mastered the art of car sales, and nothing was changing. I wasn't challenging myself anymore – I wasn't growing."

"Wait, you were selling cars?" Amusement sparked in her eyes. "You were a used car salesman?"

"A new car." Why was I blushing? "Saleswoman."

"I suppose that's why you don't seem sleazy or crooked."

A compliment? From Margo? I'd take it. "I'm just persuasive."

"I can see that." Her eyes danced over me again. "It might be nice to have you around later in the summer, when I'll be selling at the farmers market."

It was only May now, and I knew the market wouldn't start until August. Even if I stayed the full three months, I'd be gone by then.

"It's just a shame you can't persuade goats into giving you milk," she said.

"I'm working on it." I gave her a small smile. "I'm sure I'll be able to manage it soon."

"We'd best get out there, then."

She brought her plate over to the sink and washed it while I quickly downed my last few bites of toast. As I watched her back, I felt oddly warm toward her. It seemed kind of like I'd just taken a test - and passed it.

My optimism lasted until I sat down on the stool beside Harmony. She hadn't gotten the memo about me passing the test, and even though I tried the squeezing method Margo had shown me, the goat barely gave me any more milk than she had yesterday.

Margo crouched behind me, watching. She was close enough that I could smell whatever spicy-scented shampoo she used.

"Do you need me to show you again?" she asked.

"No, you already showed me. I just..." I tried again, squeezing the goat boob for all I was worth.

"You're closer than before, but still not quite right. Step aside, I'll show you one more time."

I tried not to pout. I was new at this - I couldn't expect to get it right away. Or even after a week, apparently.

I could feel Margo's body heat as she stepped by me to get on the stool. My pulse raced, and I massaged the back of my neck. It was strange how nervous she made me. I'd never had a paying job where I wanted to please the boss this badly. Then again, I'd never been this bad at an actual job.

I just felt so out of place here. Everything about me was wrong for farm life. Every time Margo looked at me, I felt like she was judging my hair, my clothes, my general demeanor. I normally got my shoulder-length blonde hair cut, colored, and layered every six weeks. I was pretty high-maintenance in that sense.

And the tight jeans and tank tops I'd been wearing were totally impractical. I'd already gotten my arms scraped up and sunburned more than once. Whenever I got the chance, I'd switch to loose-fitting, breezy clothes like the men's flannel shirts she always wore.

"It's like this," she said, calling my attention to her as she put both hands on Harmony's teat. "Left hand, squeeze. Right hand, squeeze."

"That's what I was doing." I took a deep breath, inhaling the scent of goat poop. I couldn't keep the frustration out of my voice.

She paused to look at me, and there was actual sympathy on her face. "It takes a while to learn. You'll get it eventually."

I tried doing it the way she'd demonstrated. It felt the exact same as it had a minute ago, and the results were the same, too. "Will I?" I let out a sigh.

"Don't get discouraged, Cherry. You're new at all of this. You don't become a pro overnight. You'll get it in time."

So now she was giving me a pep talk? This entire morning was blowing my mind. "How long did it take you?" I asked, still focusing on milking Harmony.

She chuckled. "That's not a fair comparison to make. I was born into this life. I grew up on a farm."

I should've known. She seemed completely at ease with everything she did. Could I even imagine her in the city? I tried mentally transporting her onto a subway train, hanging onto a pole, a briefcase in hand, dressed in business casual. The image made me snort.

"How long does it take your other volunteers to catch on, then?" I asked.

"Hard to say," she said pensively. "Some are faster than others. On average, it might take a month or two before I'm confident they can get it done on their own."

"A month or two?" I looked back at her in shock. "That means I'll only be useful for a third of my stay? For the first two months, I could be holding you back?"

A smile played across her lips, making her look softer. I hadn't seen her smile too often, and I had to say it was a good look on her. "First of all, you shouldn't assume you'll be slow to catch on," she chided. "There's no reason that you couldn't catch on quicker than other people."

I hadn't yet, but I let her continue.

"Secondly, you won't be holding me back. Even when I have to show you how to do something over and over, you're still the one who's doing it. That frees up my time to go and do something else. I'd have a hard time managing things on my own if you were to leave now. And this is the easy part of the season." She touched my back, and her hand lingered there for a long moment. "I'm counting on your help this season, Cherry. That means I'm fully confident that you'll learn this stuff and be able to do it on your own."

My throat was tight as she took her hand off me. The touch had felt oddly comforting. "And if I don't?"

"You will." She nodded toward Harmony. "Look at you. You're doing it."

I turned back and stared at the bucket. My hands had been working unconsciously, and there were several more inches of milk than there had been before. I slowed to a stop, unable to continue now that I was thinking this hard about it.

"And you know what else?" Margo asked. "Even if you were terrible at everything, you'd still be making a difference here. Being alone on this farm can be exhausting. Just having someone around helps a lot."

"Having someone to talk to?"

She took a moment to answer, as if she was wondering whether I'd made a jab at her. I wasn't quite sure what I'd meant, myself.

"Sure," she finally said. "Sometimes I feel so isolated, I forget how to talk. But seeing another human face, knowing another person's around - it helps."

Nodding, I squeezed Harmony's teat a few more times. The milk kept coming out - not as much as Margo could get, but more than I'd gotten before.

"You're doing about as well as I'd expect," she said softly. "You're worrying too much. You're already learning, and you're only going to get better. The fact that you're here, that you're staying, that you've committed to this - that's the most important part."

"If you say so."

She put a hand on my arm to stop me from milking. As my skin tingled where she'd touched it, she picked up the bucket and held it out to me. "This is why you're here."

I stared at her, not understanding what she wanted me to do.

"Take a sip," she said. "It's okay that it's not hygienic, you and me are the only ones who are going to drink it. Try it - see what fresh, pure, raw milk tastes like."

Slowly, I brought the bucket to my lips. The stainless steel sent a chill through me as I tilted the pail upward. It seemed a little gross to drink this so soon after it'd been inside Harmony. I took the tiniest sip that I could.

Oh… fuck. The thick, creamy liquid dissolved on my tongue, and flavours more complex than I'd ever tasted in store-bought milk diffused through my mouth.

This might just be the most delicious thing I'd ever tasted.

"This is what makes it all worth it," Margo said. "You put in the work. You made this happen. Now you get to reap the rewards. This is how I feel every time I eat a vegetable I planted or reap a field that I sowed."

I had to admit, I saw what she meant. Farm work wasn't like selling cars. It was harder and more physical, but there was a real, tangible point to it. A really damn tasty point.

And seeing the approval on Margo's face as I started to understand – that was the most satisfying part of all.

FOUR

The next few days were much more pleasant than the last few. I noticed myself becoming more comfortable with our daily tasks - milking Harmony and feeding her, watering the greenhouse and weeding the fields.

Margo still threw new things at me on a regular basis. Even with those, I was more confident. I had the sense that I'd be able to master them with enough time. I was still out of my element, but I was more at ease every day.

I'd come to see my first week here as something like a trial by fire. I'd made it through that first little while, feeling useless at everything and having to deal with Margo being cold to me. Surely I could make it through the rest of the three months - slowly learning the ropes on the farm, with Margo maybe, possibly being a little friendlier.

She talked to me more now, and she asked me questions. We didn't talk about anything particularly personal. I asked her about what we were doing, and she answered without judging me for not already knowing. We spoke more about basic things than about anything deep or meaningful.

While she wasn't the most social person, I was

starting to think that was just her personality. She seemed to be an introvert – she didn't require constant human interaction.

In general, I did – but that was in the city. Now that I was falling into the rhythms of farm life, I could feel myself calming. Things were slower here, quieter. I needed less stimulation than I usually did.

I texted Tyler every day, and we had quick phone calls when I could get reception. I spoke to my mom and my sister, too. Not so much to my friends. They'd drifted away a while ago. It'd been hard to keep in touch after what happened.

So Margo was my main source of company, which was fine. Little by little, she was showing more charm and humor – although she still intimidated the crap out of me. If her confidence and composure could rub off on me, I'd be happy.

In the field one day, we spread her homemade compost over the just-planted crops. The stuff still smelled a lot like manure, and I covered my nose with the collar of my shirt every time she looked away. I couldn't believe how much I'd spent on my cute farming outfits, only to end up using them as a handkerchief.

"Are we doing the entire farm?" I asked as she shoveled compost off the wheelbarrow and onto the lanes of dirt.

She'd told me the farm was a little over ten acres

- small for a real farm, big for a family farm. Seeing as it was only me and her, I figured ten acres was huge for two people.

"Yes, all of them." Her expression was unruffled, despite the dirt on her face. "It'll take a while, but we'll get it done."

"How can you use all of the fields in one year?" I asked, using my forearm to wipe the sweat from my brow. "Doesn't that deplete the soil, or something?" I was rather proud of myself for coming up with such an intelligent question. Maybe I did know a thing or two about farming after all.

Except that now Margo was staring at me as if the question had horrified her. "This is a permaculture farm," she said.

"A what?"

She stopped moving in order to stare at me harder. "Permaculture," she said flatly. "You know, the kind of agriculture that imitates the features observed in natural ecosystems? I don't have to rotate the crops because I use companion planting and intercropping instead."

I blinked at her, wildly confused. She'd pretty much started speaking another language. "Sorry, I have no idea what you're talking about."

"The whole point is a permanent culture - a method of growing food that's sustainable for the long term. The farm is as self-sustaining as possible. It's a closed-loop system, bringing as little in or out as possible."

Her passion for the subject was showing, and that made me want to keep her talking – even though I still didn't have a clue what she was getting at. "Okay… cool… Go on."

She spoke slower now, as if she was talking to a little kid. "On a permaculture farm, you don't need to rotate the crops because you plan what you're growing so that it won't deplete the soil. It's much better for the environment, and more sustainable in general."

"Okay." I frowned. "So on a normal farm, what I said would have been right."

"Yes, but this isn't a normal farm." She gestured with her shovel at the field around her. "Didn't you read the description of this place before you came here? I talked a lot about permaculture on the website."

"I found it in the volunteer handbook, actually. The paper copy." I grabbed my shovel and threw more smelly compost onto the ground. "I went old-school. Closed my eyes, flipped the pages, and stuck in a pin. I went with the first farm I saw." A white lie – I'd gone with the second. The first was too close to home.

"It was that random, huh?" She gave me a funny look before she picked up her own shovel and started again, too. "You must've been pretty desperate to get away."

"You could say that."

She was quiet for a moment, letting that sink in. Then: "Bad break-up?"

I looked at her sharply. Although the mid-morning sun was high, the floppy hat she wore obscured her features. I couldn't see her expression, which I would've liked to since that was the most personal question she'd asked yet.

"No," I said. "I'm seeing someone, actually. He's waiting for me at home. You've, uh, probably heard me on the phone with him."

"That's your boyfriend?" She pushed the hat up on her forehead so I could see the surprise on her face. "When you talk to him, you sound so…"

"What?"

She looked to one side, considering. "I don't know. Not romantic, I suppose."

I coughed, suddenly self-conscious. "I guess we've been together for a long time."

"Hmm." She turned back to her work, going silent in a way that told me the conversation was over. She wasn't going to ask to see a picture of him; she wouldn't want to hear the story of how we got together.

I pushed the wheelbarrow a little further along the lane, struggling to get it to move. She'd made it look so easy! As I turned another shovelful of compost onto the ground, I looked at her again. We'd had a moment of bonding, even if she hadn't gotten all giggly and girly about it. I wasn't going to let the moment slip away.

"How about you?" I called. "Are you involved with anyone?"

She snorted. "Don't you think you would've seen some sign of that by now?"

"Not necessarily. People have long-distance relationships."

"I wouldn't put up with that, and no woman I wanted to date would, either."

I froze in mid-shovel swing, her last sentence replaying in my mind. No woman? I glanced at her again, seeing her in a new light. Of course she was gay. The way she dressed, the way she talked… the fact that she was running a farm on her own… It should've been obvious from the start.

Her sexuality wasn't a big deal, of course. I knew plenty of gay people back in Omaha. Bisexual and transgender people, too. One of my coworkers at the car dealership was a gay guy, and everybody loved him. I'd even seen pictures from his wedding.

"Makes sense." I tried to sound casual, hoping Margo hadn't noticed my second of shock. "I think long distance can work for a while, but only if you know it's going to become short distance eventually. In your case, I guess whatever woman you dated would end up having to move out here."

"Precisely." She pulled her hat low over her eyes again, blocking out the sun - or blocking me out? Had I gotten too personal now?

I decided not to chance pushing her any further. I'd already made serious progress getting closer to her today - an achievement I took an inordinate amount of pride in.

It shouldn't have mattered whether she opened up to me or not. She was basically my boss - we didn't have to like each other. But something about her - the way she carried herself, or maybe just her general impressiveness as a person - made me want to know everything about her.

I was quiet as we finished composting the field, only speaking to her when necessary. Around eleven, we headed back to the house. We'd gotten in a routine of me making lunch and her making dinner. She liked to have something simple for lunch, like cold sandwiches or tortilla wraps, which meant I didn't have to use the gas stove.

Before I could get started, she gestured me into the living room. An entire wall was lined with bookshelves that I'd barely glanced at. Now she pointed at a section near the top.

"These books are about permaculture," she said. "Take a look when you have time. You're spending three months here - you should come out of it with an idea of what you actually did."

"Okay, sure. I can do that."

She was right – I really should try to learn as much as I could while I was here. I might have come here on a whim, and I might not intend to become a farmer myself, but I'd still dedicated three months of my life to being here. I should get as much as I could out of the experience.

I glanced through the rest of her books, wondering what else I could learn from them. I'd never been much of a reader, but with the poor cell signal and the unreliable electricity from her solar panels, this was probably a good time to get into the hobby.

The shelves were grouped into sections – some on local food, some on the food system in general. There was a huge amount of cookbooks, which kind of made her strong reaction to my cooking make more sense.

I ran my finger along the spines, reading each title. Naturally, Margo had a bunch of books on sustainable building and green living in general. There were books on spirituality and meditation, and then a bunch on yoga and fitness. She had a small section for fiction – mostly high fantasy with a few historical thrown in.

"You read a lot," I said, conscious that she was still standing behind me. "You've really read all of these?"

"No, I haven't gotten around to all of them yet. I only buy books when I go to the used bookstore in town, so I stock up when I'm there."

"Some of these look interesting."

I still hadn't looked at every shelf. The next section had science books - human evolution and plant biology. I could see why Margo would be interested in that, too. They were interesting topics, and the plant stuff would help with her farming.

I bent down to check out the lowest shelf - and my heart skipped a beat.

Lesbian Nation. Sister Outsider. Sappho's Leap. A Queer History of the United States.

Okay, maybe I should've figured out she was gay a lot sooner. I kept skimming down the shelf, trying not to show my discomfort. I shouldn't have been uncomfortable. I had no issue with gay people, and I was sure Margo had no problem with straight people. This was a total non-issue... and yet I couldn't stop reading the book titles, my eyes glued to the shelf in fascination.

The further I went, the more extreme the books got. Radical feminism, lesbian separatism, and then - my breath caught in my throat.

Kink for Lesbians. Girls Love BDSM. How to Dominate A Woman. Lesbian Sadomasochism in Erotica.

My heart pounded in my ears. Margo was into

kink. She was a domme, if I assumed the third book's title was accurate. And she was still standing behind me. She knew that I knew! How was I supposed to react to this?

Slowly, I stood up, still facing the bookshelf. Maybe I could pretend I hadn't seen anything. Surely she'd be embarrassed if I acknowledged the kind of books that were there.

But no, she wasn't going to let me get away without acknowledging it. "You seem taken aback," she said dryly.

"I…" I turned to face her. Overwhelmed by the sight of her captivating eyes and mature features – the face of a domme? – I dropped my gaze to the clay floor. "I wasn't expecting to see that."

"And yet I'm sure you weren't expecting me to be interested in human evolution, either. You had a stronger reaction to my books on BDSM."

How was she so calm about this? I felt like I had when I accidentally walked in on my college roommate having sex. Meanwhile, her tone and body language were the same as they'd been all day. "I guess they seem a bit more personal," I finally mumbled.

"I don't consider it personal." The firmness of her tone made me meet her eyes again, and their light gray depths sucked me in. "Sex is a normal, healthy part of life. Kink is a way to explore it. I'm not ashamed of my tastes, nor do I believe anyone else should be."

I edged an inch further away from her – even though some deep part of me wanted to go closer. "Okay. Cool."

"I'm sorry. I've made you uncomfortable." Though still unruffled, she seemed apologetic. "I don't want you to feel sexually harassed."

"Of course." I couldn't stop staring into her light grey eyes. They held me transfixed, and I couldn't seem to say more than a word at a time.

"All right. We won't talk about this again." She handed me a paperback from higher up on the shelf. "Read this one. It's a very basic, beginner-level introduction to the farming techniques I was telling you about. You'll enjoy it."

"Sure." My hand brushed against hers as I took the book, and a strange heat filled my low belly at the contact.

"You can ask me anything you want, anytime." She waved at the small library. "I would never force my ideas on anyone – but if you're curious about any of these subjects, just let me know. I'm an open book."

I cleared my throat. I could still barely talk. "Sounds good."

I took the book and retreated to my room. I needed a little space, and I wasn't sure why.

My boss was a dominant lesbian, but that had nothing to do with me.

Did it?

Five

The book on permaculture ended up being hard to put down. I read during our lunch break and again before bed. While the subject had the potential to be dry, the author made it fascinating. Her light, humorous writing style were the perfect introduction to the ecological design principles.

Now I had a better sense of what Margo had been talking about when I asked about crop rotation, and I felt silly for not realizing this wasn't a normal, average farm. I could see some of the systems the author talked about all over this property. Margo must have designed this entire place with these ideas in mind.

"Isn't a permaculture farm supposed to be a food forest?" I asked one morning as we waded through wet grass to the greenhouse. "Where are the seven layers?"

I'd learned that a mature ecosystem, the kind that permaculture strove to imitate, should have seven layers: a canopy of tall trees, an understory of shorter shade-loving trees, a layer of shrubs, a herbaceous layer, the soil surface, the roots under the soil, and then a vertical layer of climbers and vines.

I'd been trying to line my new knowledge up with what I saw here. Margo had berry bushes for shrubs, all kinds of herbs, and then cover crops that grew close to the soil and potatoes and carrots that grew under it. She'd mentioned there were grapes and raspberries that'd grow later in the season, which I assumed counted as the vertical layer. But this farm didn't have either tall or short trees, at least not that I'd seen.

"It will be a food forest," she said, pushing the brim of her floppy hat up so she could see me. "I only started all of this eight years ago, remember? Once I decided to go off on my own, it took me a solid year just to build the Earthship. The trees have been planted, but they'll take some time to grow."

"Where are they?"

"In the ground, hon." She blinked, looking like she'd surprised herself by using the affectionate term. "You know the little plants that look woodier than the others? And then the ones that are bigger, that are spaced a few feet apart?"

I shook my head. "I'm not sure."

"All right, I'll show you."

She turned away from the greenhouse, toward a field we'd worked the other day. When it took me a moment to turn along with her, she touched my elbow to point me in the right direction.

I closed my eyes and bit my lip, overwhelmed by the heat building within me. My body responded every time Margo touched me, and it seemed like the response was greater every time. I had no idea why my body would do that. These days, nothing even happened when my actual boyfriend touched me.

We came to the edge of the field, and Margo pointed at some plants I hadn't paid attention to before. "See those? The short, leafy ones with the wooden stems? Those are pear trees. That's the canopy. The ones between them are apple trees for the understory."

I stared around the field, wondering how I'd never noticed all the trees in all the times I'd been out here. "I think I thought they were shrubs."

"You're funny, Cherry." She touched my arm again - only to direct my attention to another plant, but it affected me all the same. "That one there is an olive tree. That's my baby. It's two years old, and it might not produce fruit for another ten years."

"Ten years?"

She laughed. "I'm going to savor those olives like I've never savored an olive before."

I shook my head. This woman was seriously impressive. Not only did she run the entire farm by herself, she'd built it from the ground up. And her advance planning was incredible. I didn't have a single item in my ten-year plan.

Then again, just a short while ago I hadn't known if I'd be around in ten years.

"What are you thinking?" she asked softly. "Your face just went all serious."

"Nothing." I wasn't going to think about things like that, and I especially wasn't going to talk about them. "I was wondering if the seedlings in the greenhouse are going to mind us being late today."

"I think they'll be all right. This little detour only took about two minutes."

"Better not risk it." I flashed her a forced grin and spun around. "We should go water them."

The plants weren't too mad at us – at least, not as much as Harmony had been the day we were late to milk her.

As the day wore on, though, I couldn't stop contemplating what my physical response to Margo might mean.

I was starved for touch, obviously. Human physical contact was necessary for a healthy life. It was only the two of us here, so there was no one else to touch me. Of course my body was going to take notice when she did.

It didn't mean I was attracted to her or anything. I'd never been interested in a woman. I'd have no issue with it if I did, but I wasn't. There was something magnetic about her, something that drew me to her – but in a respectful, admiring way, not a sexual one.

I wasn't interested that way in anyone but Tyler – my sweet, loving boyfriend who was waiting for me back at home. He hadn't crossed my mind once this morning, and now that I was thinking of him, I was having a hard time remembering the shape of his face.

As soon as we finished work for the day, I resisted the urge to dive back into my book. Instead, I picked up the phone.

Tyler sounded happy to hear from me. Happier than I was to hear from him. "I've missed you so much, babe. I've been dying to call you, but you always say the reception is so terrible."

"It is." I was tempted to lie and say that was why I hadn't called recently. The truth was, I just hadn't thought of it.

"I have so much to tell you. It seems that Joe's been seeing Andrea, and no one knew until Mike caught them making out in the parking lot after work. But Mike used to date her, so – "

I tuned out as he went on with the workplace drama. At one time, I would've been as eager to hear the gossip as he was to share it. Now, no part of me was curious. The people he was talking about felt like characters from a TV show I'd watched long ago, even though I'd been working with them up to a few months ago.

But even if I'd still known them well, the events of their lives didn't seem important anymore. It was all frivolous. Fake. The farm, the goat, the food – those were actual, tangible things. Things that mattered.

The phone line was silent, and I realized a moment too late that Tyler was waiting for me to respond. "That's crazy," I tried.

Apparently that was an acceptable answer, because he went on to talk about the scandal some more. Again, I found myself spacing out. The permaculture book had been filling my head with so many new things, real things. There was no room in there for silliness anymore.

"Anyway, what's going on with you?" Tyler finally asked.

About time he gave me a chance to talk. I launched into an explanation of the farming ideas I'd been learning about. With all the benefits of organic food, I wondered how I'd ever eaten anything else.

He listened for a moment, sounding slightly bemused when he eventually interrupted me. "You're really getting into this stuff, huh?"

"Well, yeah. It's awesome." I sounded more defensive than I'd meant to.

"That's... great. I'm glad you're having fun." He sounded like he was chewing his lip. "How's the lady? Mango, was it?"

"Margo." I laughed. "She's good." She was outside reading a book on a lawn chair, so I could speak freely. "Would you believe it if I told you I found out she's a dominant lesbian?"

"What?" Now I had his interest. "How in the

world did that come up?"

I told him briefly about the bookshelf and what she'd said. "I don't think I've ever met anyone who was so open about that kind of thing. It's true, though, sex is just a part of life."

"Or she was hitting on you."

I sputtered. "No. No, I don't think so."

"It sure sounds like it."

"She was just being open and honest. It wasn't like that."

"I doubt that. The day you arrived must've been like Christmas for her. A sweet young thing walking straight into her house..."

"Oh, stop." I was oddly flattered by the idea, even though I knew it wasn't true. "She doesn't see me like that. She probably likes mature, accomplished women. Women more like her."

"I bet she wouldn't kick you out of bed for eating crackers."

"She isn't into me."

A note of concern came into Tyler's voice. "You seem pretty concerned with whether she likes you. Are you..."

"No!" I burst out, not waiting for him to finish. "I'm straight, remember? And I'm not submissive, either. I couldn't be less interested in her if I tried."

"All right," he said warily. "You know, you

have this whole new lease on life… you're trying new things… Most girls seem to be at least a little bi-curious. It wouldn't be too much of a leap for you to want to try a dominant woman, too."

"I wouldn't!" Even if my skin was prickling up in goosebumps at the very idea.

"Okay, babe. But if you ever do want to explore anything with her, I'm fine with it."

"What?"

We'd never talked about opening our relationship in any way, shape, or form. We'd been exclusive to each other for the past three years. Now he was going to throw this bomb at me as if it was any other casual thought?

"I can't be there with you," he said. "You shouldn't have to stay celibate the whole time. Besides, I think it would be hot."

I rubbed a hand over my face. "I don't want to explore anything with anyone but you. You feel the same, don't you? Or are you having problems staying celibate for three months?"

"Not at all," he said - maybe a little too quickly.

He changed the subject immediately. We spoke a little while longer, but the whole time, I was still thinking about what he'd said.

What he'd said about the idea being hot bothered me in ways I couldn't explain. Margo was so amazing in so many different ways. Her mere existence was a million miles beyond his limited understanding of "hotness." And then when I thought about the kinky aspect of it all... Even without knowing the details myself, I was pretty sure Tyler couldn't even begin to conceptualize what could happen between me and her.

Too late, I realized the line had gone silent again. "Are you still thinking about it?" he asked eagerly. "About her?"

"No," I snapped. "Stop asking."

"Okay."

"Seriously, Tyler, your whole attitude right now is grossing me out. If I ever had sex with a woman, it would be for me. Not for you to get all horny and jerk off over it." I'd called him by his name, not "babe," so he'd know I was serious.

"I didn't say I was going to jerk off over it!" he protested.

"I don't care. Women like Margo don't exist to fuel your stupid straight-guy fantasies. She's a person, not some fucking sex toy."

"All right, all right."

He didn't sound like he got it. "You saying I can sleep with her offended me. I'm not going to have sex with anyone else, male or female. Sex with a woman is just as real as any other sex."

"Okay, Cherry. Whatever. I'm going to go." His

voice was exasperated – as if he was the one being put upon. "And if you ever want to hook up with her, I still don't mind. I'm not saying to go do it. I'm just saying not to hold back because of me."

"Fuck, Tyler, did you not hear anything – "

Before I could finish the sentence, he'd hung up.

Six

I wished I had someone to vent to about Tyler's obnoxiousness. I couldn't talk about sexual topics with my mom - she had the complete opposite of Margo's sex-positive attitude. My sister was less of a prude, but it was weird to tell her about dirty stuff. Since my friends had gotten so distant from me over the past year, they weren't an option, either. And I certainly wasn't going to vent to Margo herself.

So I tried not to think about what Tyler had said, even as I was painfully conscious that he wasn't texting or calling me. Several days passed before I heard a single word from him, and it literally was a single word. Hey.

I tossed my phone aside, intending to reply to him later. There was nothing I wanted to say to him at the moment.

Margo and I had been talking more and more, often touching on the different subjects I'd seen on her bookshelf - farming and green living and sustainability. We'd delved a little into spirituality, and she told me she meditated for half an hour before I woke up every morning. I'd been here for a month and I'd had no idea. I was in awe.

"So you just turn your brain off?" I asked. "How

do you not fall asleep?"

She chuckled. "Some people call meditation a conscious sleep. It certainly refreshes me as much as a good nap does."

"How did you even learn to do that?"

"Like many things, Cherry, it just takes practice." Her gray eyes glittered at me.

I tipped the watering can over the artichoke seedlings. The greenhouse was warm today, and I was pretty sure we'd be bringing all the plants in it outside soon. "The way I learned to water plants?"

I'd nearly drowned a lot of seedlings when I'd first come here – and when Margo had caught me and corrected me, I'd switched to nearly parching them instead.

"Exactly," she said.

We finished up and headed back to the house. "I'm going into the city this Saturday afternoon," she told me as she washed her hands. "I go every month or two to pick up supplies. You're welcome to come if you'd like, or you could stay here. It's a two-hour drive, so you'd have to fend for yourself if – "

"No, I want to go. That sounds great." I hadn't been off this farm in forever. I honestly felt like a different person from when I'd shown up. The soil was seeping into my brain.

"Okay," she said, moving aside so I could use

the sink. "It can be a little break for you - you can explore the city, or do whatever you'd like. Get a massage, maybe. You've been going nonstop since you got here."

She'd worked every weekend since I'd been here. Some of the farm tasks absolutely had to be done every day, like feeding and milking Harmony. I wasn't selfish enough to sit around and chill while she took everything on - plus there was nothing more interesting to do around here - so I'd worked, too.

"That's all right." I shook my hands dry. "My back is young. It can handle this stuff."

"Get a haircut, then, maybe." She tugged on a strand of my hair.

My heartbeat spiked. That touch had been unnecessary - so why had she done it? It had to mean she was at least fond of me, if not attracted to me. And I was only hoping for the fondness.

"Is my hair that bad?" I asked, my voice coming out breathier than I'd intended it to.

"Not at all." She patted my cheek as she - finally - let go of my hair. "Just an idea for you to relax. Lately you seem wound up tight."

Were my issues with Tyler that obvious? I couldn't believe someone I'd known for so little time could read me so well.

"What kind of stuff are you going to get in town?" I asked, blatantly changing the subject. "Some fancy new seeds or tools?"

"No, I get that kind of thing shipped in the mail. When I go into town, it's for something much more important. Something time-sensitive, that wouldn't survive the drive out here without special preparations."

I stared at her as she moved toward the stove. She made it sound like she was a top-secret spy. "James Bond much?"

Her tongue darted out to wet her lips, and she raised her eyebrows as if she was about to share a secret. "I'm talking about ice cream."

"Oh, my God." My eyes nearly rolled out of my head. "You got me."

"No, I'm serious!" Her laugh was louder, freer than I'd ever heard it before. "It's my biggest vice. The grocery delivery services don't go this far into the boonies, and as many times as I've tried with goat milk, homemade just isn't the same as the store-bought stuff. I have a cooler for my trips into town, and if I pack it with ice, it keeps everything fresh until I can get it back here and into the freezer."

"I guess that makes sense." I shook my head. "I had no idea you were so into ice cream."

"I've been having cravings." The way she looked at me from beneath her lashes made my cheeks flush.

I turned away abruptly to put plates on the table, and the noise from her end told me she was getting ready to cook. "What else is in town?" I asked.

"I do have some other things to pick up. Rice, spices, supplies. They're just less exciting."

"I mean, do you get massages? See friends? Anything like that?" I glanced back at her over my shoulder. "Do you have friends?"

She looked mildly offended. "Yes, I have friends. You'll meet some eventually. They visit me here."

I wondered if they'd be the same kind of people as her. Farmers? House builders? Incredibly attractive? Wildly intelligent?

"What about dating?" I pressed. "Can't you meet women in the city? Surely there must be someone that'd be willing to come out here every weekend."

She stopped moving. "It's not a priority for me right now." She pursed her lips, then let out a sigh. "I might as well be honest with you. I moved to the city when I was younger – probably around your age. I wanted to go to college and live the kind of life I saw on TV. I was raised in this kind of environment. My parents were back-to-the-land types, hippies, if you want to put it that way. I wanted to try something new… to see if I could succeed in the real world."

She'd dropped her guard, at least for the moment. She'd never opened up to me like this before, and my eyes were wide as I listened.

What else might she be willing to tell me? I wanted to know everything. If I could figure out the right question to ask, I'd have the answers I wanted so badly.

"And then what happened?" was the best I could come up with.

"I did a year at the college in Boise," she said slowly. "I studied agriculture - you'd think it'd be a perfect fit, right? It wasn't. They focused on industrial farming, the kind of commercial farms that are focused only on profit at the expense of the environment. When I spoke about sustainability, I was jeered at and mocked. Even organic farming was practically unheard of at the time, and my personal beliefs go a lot farther than that."

I nodded, making a mental note to ask her more about that later. I could tell she was slowly getting around to what I'd asked her about, circuitously making her way to the point.

"While I was there, I did meet a girl," she said. "A woman, I suppose I should say - but at the time, we both felt like girls. We were so young, and everything was new and exciting. Her name was Jasmine."

Her expression went dreamy as she spoke about the girl. A spark of jealousy shot through me, and I quickly extinguished it. It was good to see Margo's human side, and to get this insight into her past. I wasn't going to ruin this moment with silly, senseless emotions.

"We dated for most of that year," she went on. "I thought it would last forever. Everything was so perfect, I couldn't see how it could ever end. We fit together like two puzzle pieces slotting into place. She completed me. And then..."

She sighed, closing her eyes briefly in clear pain. "I decided to drop out of school and come back here. For a while, we thought we'd make it work. Jasmine said she'd visit me and I'd visit her, and we'd overcome the distance until she graduated and she could move out here. She was so convincing - or maybe she really believed what she was saying, I still don't know.

"We lasted about a month apart, and then she called and confessed she'd met somebody else. And that wasn't all - she didn't think she would've been able to move out here. She was a city girl." The words dripped with bitterness. "She wouldn't have been able to give that up - to let her whole life go. She was perfectly suited for me in every way, but only as long as I was forcing myself to be something I wasn't. As soon as I came back here, back to myself, she was gone."

I took a silent breath, waiting for her to continue. She didn't - it seemed like her story was over. That was all I was going to get out of her today.

"I'm sorry, Margo," I said. "I understand everything much better now."

"That's all right." She shook her head. "Anyway, that's why I'm not fussed about meeting somebody. I know people like me, who want to live this kind of way, are rare. I don't expect to meet anyone I can have a serious relationship with. Of course, that doesn't mean I'm permanently celibate. I've had casual relationships, and they were perfectly pleasurable."

For some reason, my mind chose that moment to picture her eating ice cream, her eyes fluttering shut in enjoyment, her tongue scooping a melted drop from the corner of her mouth. I pictured her looking for ice cream recipes, collecting Harmony's milk, blending the ingredients together, sliding the bowl into the freezer, all in the anticipation of that moment of pleasure…

"What kind of girl do you go for?" I blurted out. "What's your type?"

"I wouldn't say I have one." Her eyes lingered on me. "Not in terms of physical traits."

"What, then?" My heart was beating faster again – my body knew I was treading down a dangerous path.

"I'm attracted to women who are willing and eager to submit." Her voice was low, meaningful. "To me, specifically."

I was still holding onto the glasses I'd been putting on the table, and I stood frozen with them in my hands until I realized what I was doing. Letting go, I massaged the back of my neck.

"So that's the most important thing to you," I said. "More than age, looks, life accomplishments..."

"Compatibility is always the most important, yes." Her gaze followed my hands as I moved them awkwardly to my sides. "But there are many different aspects to compatibility."

Silent, I straightened the edge of a placemat that was already straight.

"Why do you ask, Cherry?"

That was what I'd feared she'd ask - and I didn't know how to answer. "No reason," I said after a long pause. "Just curious."

"Yes, many people are," she said softly. "Curious, that is."

Gathering my courage, I met her eyes again. She was leaning on the counter now, her food preparations apparently forgotten. It seemed like our conversation was more interesting to her. And I had no idea how to deal with that.

"What's on your mind?" Her gray eyes held me transfixed. "What are you thinking?"

"My boyfriend..." I shook my head. "He's an asshole."

"Why?"

"He made this stupid remark - that if I wanted to explore anything - with you - " I couldn't look at her anymore. For this part, I turned away. "He thought that would be hot."

"I see." Her voice was steely.

I peeked over at her again. "I told him to go to hell, obviously. That was way out of line."

"Because you wouldn't be interested? Or because it was disrespectful to me?"

"I..."

I couldn't say no to the first question. I had no clue how or why, but the idea wouldn't leave me alone. Now that she was speaking openly about it, the thought of it possessed me. I didn't know exactly how it would work, exactly what she'd do, but already I could practically feel the chill of handcuffs around my wrists - and the thrum in my low belly begged me to make it real.

But I couldn't say yes. Partly because I was straight and it'd never work. But to my surprise, that was becoming less and less of an issue. The main problem was - what if I told Margo about my growing fantasies, and she rejected me?

Because she had every reason to. I was basically her employee, so it'd be entirely inappropriate. And besides that, I was far too young and naïve for her to ever take an interest in me. If compatibility was the only thing that mattered to her, I was an unknown quantity. I had no idea how I'd fare at submitting to anyone, female or male.

On top of everything, I'd never delved into casual sex before. And that was all it could be.

Even if I became one of those girls who experimented with other girls, I wasn't going to marry one.

Margo's eyes glowed at me. She was still waiting for an answer.

"The second one," I mumbled. "It was out of line because it was disrespectful to you."

"Good." Her approval was immediately evident. "I'm glad you understand that." She grabbed her steak knife again - if she was going back to cooking, that meant she was about to end the conversation. "And if you ever decide you'd like to try, I would expect you to be single first."

I gaped at her. "What?"

"If you ever decide you'd like to try..." She chopped a carrot, completely unflustered.

"No, I heard you. I..."

"I told you before. If you have questions, you're welcome to ask me anytime. You can also pick up any of the books from the shelf." Shrugging, she pushed the chopped carrot aside and reached for another. "I would suggest one or the other before you make any decisions."

I was still gaping as hard as before. "Are you saying that... that kind of... experience... would be on the table?"

"Anything is on the table, if you put it there." She scraped the carrots into a bowl and set them in front of me. "Like salad... or anything else."

SEVEN

The car trip to the city was quiet. Margo had insisted she'd drive the whole way, despite me repeatedly offering to give her a break. She didn't want to play any music, either.

I sat in the passenger seat, flicking through the pages of the green living book I'd borrowed from her "library." I wasn't as interested in it as I'd been in the permaculture one - maybe because I kept wondering why I'd picked this instead of one of the books on BDSM.

That was where my mind kept going. I thought about what Margo had said every day - probably every hour. I didn't know much about any kinky things. I'd read 50 Shades, of course, and giggled my way through the movie. I knew everyone said that was "bad" BDSM - but what would it mean for BDSM to be good?

It was odd - at this point, I wasn't even concerned about the gender issue anymore. Margo was captivating enough that gender was irrelevant. I was drawn to her in a way I was powerless to even try to prevent. I may not have understood that, but I was starting to accept it.

"How's your book?" she asked, changing lanes to pass another car on the highway.

"It's okay. I can't really get into it."

"Not as good as the last one? I could've recommended you another."

"I guess I should've asked you."

The main reason I'd chosen this one was that it was a hardcover, and larger than most other books. I'd had vague thoughts about sneaking a BDSM book out when Margo wasn't around and hiding it inside this one's pages.

That would've been silly, of course. Margo was so straightforward, and here I was thinking about playing games like that, like a little kid. But I didn't have the guts to be straightforward - not when it came to something like this.

You got through the whole last year, I told myself. A little lesbian BDSM should be a breeze.

But I couldn't quite manage to convince myself.

"Anything you want to ask me?" Margo asked. "About green living, or… anything else."

"Um. Well." I squirmed in my seat, feeling heat rise in my core. If I didn't broach this topic now, I'd never find the nerve for it. "How does it work when you BDSM with someone? I mean, how do you start? Do you make the girl sign a contract, like in 50 Shades?"

"Oh, goodness. Tell me that isn't your only exposure to the lifestyle."

Ashamed of myself, I nodded. But Margo's eyes were kind when she glanced over at me.

Although she seemed annoyed, it wasn't with me.

"Typical," she snorted. "The entire generation's conception of the lifestyle is contaminated."

"Why do you keep calling it 'the lifestyle'?"

"Because it's more than a fetish - at least for some of us." She tapped her fingernails on the wheel distractedly. "It doesn't necessarily have to stay in the bedroom. It really depends on the person, but for some who are serious about it, it can be a twenty-four-seven activity."

"I guess that's what I'm asking," I said. "How does it work for you in particular?"

"I prefer to keep the domination games in the bedroom - although I do enjoy being obeyed outside of it as well." She glanced over at me again. "Other than that, let's see... I don't share. That's the first thing you should know. If someone is mine, then she's mine."

"I got that much already."

It was insane that I was even thinking about ending things with Tyler over this - a casual fling with someone seventeen years my senior - a woman, to boot.

And yet, if I was considering ending things, didn't that mean they might already be over? If I was happy with Tyler, I wouldn't have given Margo a second look, no matter how seductive she was.

Tyler and I had only had a few phone calls over the past month, and each one felt more forced and awkward than the last. We weren't getting along like we used to, and that had a lot to do with the shift in my priorities since I'd come to Margo's farm.

But the more I thought about it, the more I wondered if that change had happened even before I went away. He'd been at my side through all the shit of the past year. Somewhere along the line, had he stopped seeing me as a partner and started seeing me as a project?

I cared about him, and I knew he cared about me. Sometimes, though, that wasn't enough.

Beside me, Margo went on with her list. "I wouldn't necessarily want to sign a contract with a partner. It's a little overly formal, although it wouldn't be a bad idea. The main thing would simply be to establish clear expectations and boundaries before anything happened between us."

"Why?"

"To be sure that we're on the same page," she said. "I'm not a sadist, you understand. I'll spank a woman, even paddle her, but I won't do much more than that. I'm a loving dominant, not a cruel one."

A loving dominant - wasn't that an oxymoron? I'd never heard of such a thing before.

"For example, one of my boundaries is causing

physical injury or harm," she said. "I won't do it, no matter how much my submissive wants it. I almost dated a woman, but at the early stages, I found out she loved blood play and wanted me to make her bleed on a regular basis. We clearly weren't compatible, so we ended things there and went on our way."

Both of my eyebrows rose. Margo had just made me want to ask about a million more questions. Who was this woman? Why did she want to be cut so much? Why was Margo so determined not to hurt her? And if they liked each other in every other way, why would that difference make them want to throw the whole relationship out?

"What are your other preferences?" I settled on asking.

"I like to care for my submissive." A smile tugged at the corners of her plush red lips. "Pleasing her, making her happy, is the most important thing in the world to me. Sometimes she doesn't know what's best for her, and I have to set down rules to keep her in line. In return for all I do for her, I expect her to listen and obey me - in and out of the bedroom."

"Give me an example." My voice shook slightly. "Something you'd expect."

She didn't hesitate, apparently not even needing to think about her answer. "I might tell my sub not to orgasm for a certain amount of time, knowing that the orgasm she had after waiting would be so much better than a normal one."

"And if she orgasmed anyway?"

The tremor in my voice was audible now. It was starting to hit me that as we were speeding down the highway, we were discussing the ins and outs of a potential BDSM relationship.

"Then I would have to punish her," she said. "Nothing horrible. The punishment might even be, in a way, enjoyable. But I'd need to show her that my orders aren't something to ignore."

"What if you told me – I mean, your sub – something crazy? Like, if you ordered her to chop off her arm?" My pulse raced, and sweat trickled into my armpits. I hadn't intended to refer to this hypothetical conversation actually being about me and her.

As usual, she seemed calm. I guessed this whole thing was a lot less new and scary to her than it was to me. But also, she was always calm in everything she did. Nothing ever seemed to faze her.

"If I were to order my sub to be harmed in a permanent and irreversible manner, I would not be mentally competent to be a domme," she said, as casual as if she had this discussion every day. "In fact, I'd say my sub's job would then be to care for me until if and when my mental faculties returned."

I nodded. That kind of made sense. Then again, how was I supposed to know if her mental faculties were gone? Other than in an extreme case like if she asked me to chop off my arm.

"Don't worry." She reached over to pat my hand, setting off a cascade of sparks throughout my body. "I can feel the nervousness radiating off you. If you decide you'd like to go down this path, I'll be at your side every step of the way. I'm experienced and knowledgeable."

"You sound like you're selling your skills at a job interview."

She chuckled. "I do have references."

Another spark went through me - of jealousy this time. Ironic, seeing as I was the one who was in a relationship. But I had a feeling that wasn't going to last much longer. Maybe I wouldn't have come to that realization right now without Margo in the picture, but I would've gotten there sooner than later.

Her hand lingered for a long moment on my knee, and the heat from her fingers stayed behind when she took them away. "Tell me more about what interests you in the lifestyle," she said quietly. "You wants, your needs, your expectations."

I licked my lips. "This is all new for me, you know that. I haven't thought through what I'd like and dislike."

"There must be something pulling you to it, though. The average person may be excited by the thought of whips and chains, but they shy away from actually trying it. Especially in a serious way. The fact that you've come this far means something."

My throat went dry. I hadn't thought I'd gone anywhere at all. "I don't know," I said. "I suppose I like the idea of… surrender. Of giving up control."

"Why is that?"

I didn't have a good answer for her, and that stressed me out. If I said the wrong thing, she might decide I was unfit for the lifestyle entirely, and then where would I be?

"Don't overthink it." She patted my knee again. "There are no right or wrong answers."

"You're not going to lose interest if I say something stupid?"

"I don't think that would be possible. I might realize we're not compatible, but then deciding not to pursue things would be best for both of us." She stroked my thigh. "You'd go on to find another dominant to explore things with, if you still wanted to try. Or you'd go back to your boyfriend and forget you were ever even curious."

Heat bloomed in my chest. "Okay," I said. "I guess I'd like the idea of submitting because I always want to please you. It makes me happy when you praise me. Every time you compliment me, I feel like a puppy being petted."

I was barely audible by the end. I felt utterly self-conscious. I'd stripped myself bare, been completely honest about my raw, true motivations. What would Margo do with them?

"That's good to know," Margo murmured, glancing over at me once more. "I can work with that."

"And you?" I asked, my face still blazing. "What made you want to dominate women?"

"It excites me," she said. "Having someone put their trust in me, leave their pleasure in my hands... It allows me to take care of my partner on a whole new level. BDSM is much more intimate than vanilla sex, and the rewards are greater, too."

I shivered. "Tell me more about these rewards."

She turned her blinker on, and then we were pulling off the highway, slowing down to a crawl amidst all the traffic. "That's a topic for another time," she said. "We're here."

EIGHT

Once we parked downtown, Margo set me loose to explore the city. I would've been fine tagging along with her for her errands, especially the ice cream. I would've liked to see her face when she opened a carton and tasted the chilly sweetness of her favorite flavor for the first time in months.

But she said I should take some time to be on my own. I suspected she was doing more than buying ice cream, and that she might not want company for some of her other errands. She could even be meeting up with an ex – a thought that sent a spark of jealousy flaring through me.

I didn't ask, although I was sure she would've told me. She was honest above all else.

Since I wasn't with her, I made my way through the city of Green Root on foot. Calling it a city was being generous, actually. I'd never noticed this place on a map. The sign when we entered said the population was two hundred thousand. Still, compared to Margo's farm, it felt like I'd re-entered civilization.

The downtown was about two blocks in each direction, and the buildings were one or two stories high. I'd already decided not to bother getting my hair done. Margo was the only one who'd see it, and she'd probably be more impressed if it wasn't super fancy. My brown roots were already growing in, and I didn't mind one bit.

I made a circuit around the downtown, then headed to McDonalds for a Big Mac. I hadn't eaten greasy fast food once since I got to Margo's. Inside, I sat down at one of the familiar plastic tables. Everything was the same at McDonalds, even out here in the middle of nowhere.

I took a big bite of my burger, then another. The meat didn't quite taste right. It was like I could taste the hormones and antibiotics the cow had been injected with. I felt like I was eating a pile of chemicals.

Frowning, I set it to the side and grabbed a fry. My stomach curdled. This wasn't right, either. Or had my tastes changed from spending a month eating only fresh, healthy food? I grabbed my Coke and tried a sip. Blech! It was sickeningly sweet, like someone had dumped a pile of sugar into the cup. How had I ever enjoyed drinking this crap on a regular basis?

I looked at my burger again. The thin bun and processed meat made my nose wrinkle. I didn't really want to eat this. I couldn't even stomach the fries. Pursing my lips, I dumped the entire contents of my tray into the trash can. I'd pick up some fruit at the grocery store if I was hungry enough. Otherwise, I'd wait to eat until I got back to Margo's, where I could have some real food.

I slid back into my chair and rested my chin in my hands. This farm experience really was changing me. Again, my thoughts went back to Tyler. At moments like this, it seemed definite - even obvious - that I needed to break up with him and move on. I wasn't the same person that I had been, and he was still his old self. He was a huge part of my past, but that didn't mean he had to play the same role in my present - or my future.

What if these changes in me weren't permanent, though? I might go back to my normal self after I got home. I might miss him, and he might've moved on by then. What if I broke things off and then regretted it? I had to be crazy for even thinking about splitting up with the man who'd been at my side through so much.

Staring into space, I went back and forth a few hundred more times. I couldn't make up my mind. Tyler was a great guy - but that didn't mean we were meant to be together. He'd been a perv about Margo - but he was a wonderful partner in other ways.

I just didn't know. Except... Margo's voice echoed in my head.

I don't share. If someone is mine, then she's mine.

If I stayed with Tyler, I'd never get to explore things with her. And... there was a lot to explore. My body tingled at the thought.

Before I could overthink this any more, I

grabbed my phone.

Tyler picked up after only two rings. "Cherry, to what do I owe the honor of hearing from you?" His voice was cold, flat.

Right, I hadn't called him in over a week. We'd barely texted, either. "I was just thinking of you," I said. "I - well - I'm sure you have some thoughts, too."

"I do," he said. "Like how I've been there for you through everything, putting your health and happiness ahead of mine for over a year. I even let you run off by yourself on some harebrained adventure, and then the moment I offer you even more freedom, you jump down my throat."

"Freedom?" My voice pitched high enough to draw some of the other diners' attention. I took a breath, willing myself to calm down. "I never asked for freedom," I hissed into the phone. "All I wanted was to be with you, only you."

"That's not what I heard in your voice," he said. "Do you think I don't know you by now? You said the words 'dominant lesbian' with such utter fascination, there was no question you wanted to experience it for yourself."

"No, I didn't." At least, I didn't think I had at the time.

"We're apart, and you were curious. I figured, what was the harm?" He scoffed. "I didn't think I'd get attacked for that. It's nice that you're calling to apologize – "

"Who said I was apologizing?" I sat up straight, my face hot. "I don't see how I have anything to apologize for. You've given me a little more context for what you said, but I still think it was disrespectful and wrong."

"Disrespectful? To who?"

"To Margo," I said. "And to me."

"Margo." He said her name like it was a curse. "I never thought you'd be more worried about some woman you just met than about me."

"She's not some woman. She's the most amazing person I've ever known."

"Is that so? I suppose you're sleeping with her now, aren't you? That's why you're all up in her ass all of a sudden."

"I'm not, actually. She wouldn't even consider it while I was still seeing someone. That's the kind of person she is." My voice went steely. "And if I was, I wouldn't tell you anyway. I know you'd just be gross about it."

"So she's amazing and I'm the devil. I get it." He sounded just as mad as me now. "I hope she's the kind of person who'll spend every day taking care of you when you're not well. Hold your hand while you're crying. Support you in every decision you make, even when it means letting you leave for three months."

"I appreciate everything you did for me, Tyler. I

do. But – "

"Go fuck yourself, Cherry."

With limp hands, I lowered the phone. The screen read "Call Ended."

So that was done. It was over. I pressed my face into my hands, conscious that people were looking at me. At least they were strangers and I'd never see them again.

A tear spilled down my cheek, through my fingers. I knew – well, I was pretty sure – that I'd done the right thing. Still, my three-year relationship had just ended. In the middle of a McDonalds.

Collecting myself, I got up. The other people in the place looked away from me, although they snuck a few peeks as I walked out. This had to be the most excitement they'd seen all day, in a town like this.

I checked the time. I had an hour and a half until I was supposed to meet Margo, and I was probably still going to be a mess then. I walked around the streets, trying to enjoy the warm spring air, but all I could think about was Tyler.

At the end of one street, a small, dingy sign indicated there was a used bookstore. An arrow pointed to stairs that led below street level. Despite my aching heart, I smiled. That seemed like a decent way to kill a little time. Margo's library was so extensive that I could read from it for months. Still, I was reading more these days than ever before in my life. It'd be fun to find a book of my own.

As I stepped down the stairs, I wondered if she knew about this place. Surely she did – she came to Green Root regularly – but then, this place was somewhat hidden. She might be surprised if I told her about it. She might be happy.

An elderly man sleepily welcomed me to the store. I looked around the dusty shelves, wondering where to start. There was a whole section on the environment. That could be good – I didn't know much about it, and living with Margo was making me want to get informed.

I tilted my head to scan through the books' titles, the way I did at her place. Environment and Ethics – that could be interesting. Probably more up her alley than mine. I traced my finger along the spines as I walked down the row. So You're Off the Grid – Now What? Laughing out loud, I picked it up.

I browsed for a while longer, accumulating more books as I went. By the time I glanced at my watch again, I'd amassed five books – all of them for Margo. As I paid, I tried to remember why I'd been upset when I came in here. Oh, right – Tyler. I hadn't thought of him since I came in.

I walked out of the bookstore with a spring in my step. Things were going to be okay – especially with Margo. Now that I was single, I could explore and experiment to my heart's content.

And I didn't feel at all like I'd thrown away a healthy, loving relationship for "some woman I'd just met." The relationship was over, with or without Margo. And whatever happened between us would just be for the thrill of it. I'd be single when I got back to Omaha, and that was absolutely fine. I'd think about dating then - maybe guys, maybe girls, maybe both. I didn't know. I'd cross that bridge when I came to it.

I found Margo in the parking lot of the grocery store. She was crouched halfway inside the car, and I swallowed hard as I checked out her round, soft-looking ass. I'd never ogled a woman before her, and yet there was something familiar about it. Maybe I'd been doing it unconsciously all my life.

"Hey there," I said when she got out. "You got your ice cream?"

"Yeah, a cooler full of it." She gestured at the car, and I saw she'd buckled the cooler into the seat like a child. "I already had a cup. It was magnificent."

"You take your ice cream seriously." I laughed. "Um, these are for you, by the way."

Raising her eyebrows, she took the books I offered her. "You got me books? You didn't have to!"

"I just felt like it." I shrugged. "I mean, they're ones I wanted to read, but I figured I won't have room to take them with me, and they seemed like ones you'd like – that's if you don't have them already, and I didn't remember seeing them – "

"Cherry. Stop overthinking this. It's a lovely gift." Touching my arm, she leaned in and kissed me on the cheek.

My cheeks heated instantly, and the spot where her lips had touched me burned. My core thrummed for more. How had she had that effect on me? God, it was only a kiss on the cheek!

One thing was clear – I definitely wasn't as straight as I'd always thought.

"I'm glad you like it," was all that I said.

"You're turning into a reader, like me. Soon you'll be a book hoarder, too."

"Or maybe that's why I'm pawning them off on you."

Shaking her head, she turned her attention to the books. "So You're Off the Grid – Now What?" she read, and laughed. "Sounds perfect for me. Oh, Eco Living for Feminist Freaks. Thanks a lot!"

I fought the urge to touch my cheek where she'd kissed it. "I thought you might be into it."

"Anarcho-Primitivism for Dummies," she went on, looking at each book in the stack. "Natural Healing Methods… oh… The Sensual Dance of

Submission." Her eyes flickered to mine, and she gave me a small nod. "I like that one."

"It's more for me, but I thought you might get something out of it." I coughed, unable to hold her gaze. "I guess we should get going if we want to milk Harmony on schedule."

"I guess you're right."

We got back on the road, and she yawned as she merged onto the highway. It was nearly empty this far into the country, and she quickly sped up to ninety miles an hour. I stretched my legs as far as they could go, flicking through the pages of the books I'd bought.

"Oh, I broke up with Tyler," I said offhandedly.

The car jerked, making both of us curse. Margo slowed slightly, easing the car between the lines again. When she'd recovered, she looked at me sharply. "You did what?"

"I broke things off." She sounded less pleased than I'd expected, and I wondered if I'd made a terrible mistake. What if she didn't want to do anything with me after all? What if I'd misinterpreted everything she'd said about BDSM?

"That seems sudden." She glanced in the rear view mirror, her features hard with concern. "Are you sure that's what you want?"

"I'm sure. I was reaching the point where I would've wanted to break up with him anyway, even if… if…"

"Even if you weren't hoping to be my submissive," she finished for me. "You're going to have to get a lot more comfortable talking about kink."

I nodded self-consciously. The problem wasn't the kink, it was the assumption that it was going to happen with her. I still couldn't quite make myself believe it.

"I'm happy for you, then," she said. "I'm certainly happy for myself."

I wriggled in my seat, wondering what exactly she'd be happy about - what she wanted to do to me.

"So we're going to do this, then?" I asked quietly.

Her eyes slid over to me, then returned to the road. "You're with me for almost two more months. You just had a break-up. You'll probably need some time to recover, or – "

"No." I didn't hesitate. Didn't have to think about it. "I want to start now."

Nine

It turned out that when it came to Margo, "now" didn't mean "now."

When we got back to the farm, she told me she needed to interview me before we did anything kinky or sexual.

"I thought we did that on the car ride there," I said, disappointed. I'd been getting more and more aroused on the way back, thinking about all the things that might happen between us.

"That was more of an informal chat," she said. "I won't proceed without a proper interview - a sit-down session where we establish what we're going to do." A slow smile crept over her face. "I have ways to make the interview interesting."

I extended my wrists to her as if she had a pair of handcuffs stashed in her purse. "Let's do it now, then."

Her smile turned predatory, and she looked like she was tempted to bend me over and spank me there and then. But she pushed my hands back to my sides. "I love the enthusiasm… but work doesn't stop because of kink. Your first task is to go milk Harmony."

"Yes, Mistress." I gave her a wink.

I was on a high from my own cheekiness the

whole time I was in the barn. I couldn't believe I'd called her Mistress. Had she liked it? I definitely had. Would she want me to call her that all the time now?

After finishing up, I headed back into the house. Margo was in the kitchen, standing over the stove. "I took over your dinner duties for tonight," she said. "Eat something, then shower… and put on the outfit I laid out for you."

My heart jumped into my throat. She was picking things for me to wear? That just made this so much more real. I was going to do everything she said… cater to her every whim. But then, if it was too much for me, I'd tell her during our "interview." This went both ways. She was supposed to cater to me, too.

At least this should be more pleasant than the interview we'd originally had before we met. I'd called her out of the blue and told her I was hoping to come and stay with her. She'd asked me a bunch of questions, and I'd stuttered out vague half-answers. I'd thought she thought I was a bumbling idiot, but in the end she'd surprised me by saying I could come.

Then I'd shown up, and I'd still felt like she thought I was a bumbling idiot. I remembered it so clearly. I took the bus to the nearest town, and then a taxi dropped me off here. She'd been so intimidating - tall, rugged, gorgeous. She'd scanned me up and down as if evaluating me, and she'd clearly found me wanting. I had no idea why she hadn't put me on the next bus home.

After I ate and showered, I found the outfit she'd left on my bed - a soft white cotton shift, sleeveless and plain. I held it up, wondering why she'd chosen it when it didn't seem all that sexy. It looked like something you might get for a buck or two at a thrift shop.

Shrugging, I dropped my towel and slipped the dress on. One glance in the mirror, and I understood Margo's line of thinking. The dress clung to my curves like a glove, while still being loose enough to give some semblance of modesty. I could've been on my way to a tennis match or a day at the races - except that the fabric was also so sheer I could see my nipples straight through it. They hardened as I thought about her looking at them.

Maybe I should put on a bra. Panties. Those would help me feel a little more covered up. Then again, she hadn't left them out for me - and more than anything else, I wanted to please her.

Foregoing the underwear, I tiptoed to the stairs. I fought the urge to cover my breasts when I found myself in front of her. She was going to see all of me soon enough - there was no need to be modest.

Her tongue darted over her lips as her eyes slid up and down my body. She seemed to like what she saw, and that reaction made the pulse between my legs quicken. My doubts about her being into me were starting to vanish. As far as I could tell, she wanted to dominate me as much as I wanted to submit to her.

"That dress looks perfect on you," she said. "I knew it would."

"Thank you, Mistress. I love it."

"Don't get too attached." She lifted an eyebrow. "I might cut it off you at some point."

Shivering, I put my hands on the back of a chair to steady myself. Never in my life had I done anything that kinky, and Margo was talking about it as a jumping-off point.

"Let's go sit on the porch," she said. "We've never sat there together, so the new location will separate this from a normal conversation."

I followed her outside, my heart pounding more with every step. She seemed so sure of herself – why couldn't some of that confidence transfer over to me? I had no idea what I was doing. I only knew I felt compelled to do it.

I sat on one of the wicker chairs, and the evening breeze blew over us. The sun was low in the sky, and the fading light made her look more attractive than ever.

Her eyes flickered at me. "I forgot something." The tone of her voice said she hadn't forgotten, had planned it this way.

Either way, she moved behind me and affixed a

scrap of dark fabric over my eyes. I tried to breathe, but found that I couldn't. All I could see were dim shapes and outlines, none of which were Margo. She stood behind me, and her hands landed on my shoulders.

"Is this all right for you, Cherry?" Her breath made goosebumps prickle up on my ear.

"Mm-hmm." I was nervous, and yet I liked this. My nipples were so hard they had to be poking right through the white dress, and the silkiness of the blindfold made my core pulse with need.

"I want you to relax." She kneaded my muscles, digging into the tense flesh. "Just talk to me. There's nothing to be scared of."

"I'll try."

"Tell me what turns you on, Cherry." She pressed down on my shoulders, making me conscious I'd been holding them up.

"I… I don't know. I guess…" No one had asked me this before, at least not so blatantly. My exes had all assumed they turned me on, and hadn't put much thought into it than that. "I think submitting is going to turn me on… but I know you want more detail than that. Um…"

"Take your time." She moved on to my neck, using long strokes to ease the tension out of it.

"I think I like calling you Mistress." The words sounded silly when they came out, and I was embarrassed I'd even said them.

"That's a good start. Go on. You can say anything you want."

I swallowed. "I'm turned on when you tell me to do things. Like, things around the farm. And, um, I like it when you're mad at me and then you relent a little. I like it when you're nice to me, but it's even better after you were mean."

She hadn't been yelling at me as often since that first week – since she overheard me on the phone with Tyler, since she realized I was going to stay, since we started connecting as people. Still, she got mad now and then. Although I'd gotten better at farm stuff in general, I often managed to find ways to fuck up.

"You have a real thing for authority, don't you?" she asked.

Heat rose to my cheeks. "I guess I do."

"I bet a teacher-student fantasy would really get you going."

"Maybe." I blushed harder.

"It's not a bad thing, my sweet little Cherry. I'm just trying to figure out what makes you tick." She moved her hands back to my shoulders, which had tensed up all over again. "How about your turn-offs?"

"Well… anything, you know, wrong. Incest or bestiality or bathroom stuff. Even if it was role-playing."

"That's fine with me."

"Oh, and I'm not into any kind of butt stuff."

"Good to know." Her hands swept around my front, dancing along my collarbones - just shy of the tops of my breasts. "Now, tell me about your medical history."

I tensed up, jerking away from her instinctively. "What?" I couldn't stop myself - I pulled the blindfold off so I could stare at her.

"Your medical history." Her usual composure was ruffled. She wasn't quite gaping at me, but her eyes were wider than usual. She hadn't expected my reaction. "Some of our scenes may be intense in certain ways. I need to know your vulnerabilities in order to keep you safe - like if you have old injuries that I should work around, or if you're diabetic and might faint. High blood pressure, heart conditions, allergies... Even if you have back problems or tend to get muscle cramps, I'd like to know."

"Just those kinds of things?"

"Whatever is relevant," she said. "Anything that might affect our play together."

I licked my lips. I understood what she was saying - but I'd come here to leave my medical problems behind me, and I wasn't about to confess to them now. What bigger turn-off could there possibly be - both for me and for her?

What had happened was over. I'd made a full recovery. It wasn't going to affect me now.

"That makes sense." I settled myself back in the

chair. "Sorry, I was a little surprised. I didn't know why you'd ask, but I get it now. I can't think of anything that would be relevant. Oh, I'm allergic to penicillin, but I don't see how that would come up."

"You're sure that's all?" Her eyes searched mine.

"Yeah. Yeah, that's all. Go on with what you were doing." I pulled the blindfold back over my eyes, hoping she'd return to massaging the top of my chest. I had a feeling she'd been about to go for my breasts, and the nerve endings there cried out for her touch.

She returned her hands to my shoulders, less assuredly than before. She stood still for a moment, and then the air behind me moved. Her breath on my ear told me she'd bent to speak to me. "This won't work if you're not completely honest with me, Cherry."

My gut twisted, my arousal flagging. "I'm being honest." And I was, because what I'd gone through was over - irrelevant. "Mistress," I added.

That seemed to satisfy her, and she went back to kneading my muscles. "Tell me about your fantasies."

I thought about it for a moment, and I managed to voice a few ideas that'd filtered through my brain. But the whole time, a voice in the back of my mind worried that I was lying.

And that was hardly the best way to start off my

first BDSM relationship.

TEN

Once the interview was over, Margo told me we were done for the night, and that I should go be alone. I groaned internally. She'd gotten me all worked up with her questions, not to mention her soft, warm hands, and I wished she'd follow through on the implicit promise.

But she said we should take things one step at a time. "You're new to all of this," she told me. "I don't want to overwhelm you."

"What if I want to be overwhelmed?" I asked, staring at her plump lips. More than ever, I wanted to kiss them - and to feel them on my body.

Now that I'd admitted my attraction to a woman, it was entirely frustrating to have to wait. I liked her, she liked me - so what was the delay?

I took a deep breath and let it out as I walked away from her. Up in my room, I had nothing to do. The woman I wanted was a flight of stairs away, and it felt silly and pointless to not go down there and kiss her. But she'd explained her reasoning, and I had to accept that.

On the other hand… that didn't mean I had to stay frustrated. I took my clothes off and cozied up under the covers, closing my eyes and letting my imagination run wild as my hands drifted to my chest. I could almost convince myself the light pinches and squeezes on my nipples came from Margo.

I licked my lips, feeling the heat rise inside me. I was all hot and bothered, and all because of Margo. None of my exes had ever made me feel anything like this. Then again, none of them had put so much care and effort into my pleasure. They'd never interrogated me about my fantasies, making me name and catalogue each one.

They'd never stroked gentle hands everywhere but where I needed them, working me up until my core throbbed for more, then left me on my own to try - just try - to satisfy myself...

My hips pushed upward insistently, and I gave in to my own demands. Margo had teased me enough for one night. From now on, I was going to give myself what I needed.

The little circles I always made on my clit felt heavenly tonight. My core tightened and relaxed with every stroke I made, and my teeth sank into my bottom lip. I rubbed myself lightly, then a little harder. I wondered how Margo would touch me, when she touched me. If she'd be gentle, or a little rough...

My eyes squeezed shut as I massaged my clit more vigorously. Maybe she was outside my room now. Maybe she knew what I was doing - she'd come in any moment now. I could almost feel her bending over me, pressing her pillowy lips to mine. Could feel her pulling the blanket off me, catching a nipple between her teeth.

My movement sped up as my wetness gushed. I was working myself into a frenzy. It felt like Margo was standing over me right now. She might push my legs apart, rip my hand away… put her mouth in its place. She might straddle me, a big luscious dildo strapped between her thighs. She could push into me, take me how she wanted me, not stop until I screamed…

My hand moved frantically over my clit. My body thrashed, my arms and legs shaking as the climax took over me. I could feel Margo now - caressing my breasts, plunging inside me, whispering sensual secrets into my ear. She was on me. She was there.

Except when the waves of orgasm subsided, when I opened my eyes, she was nowhere to be found.

When the morning came, she seemed just as absent, even though she was actually there. She acted the same as usual, telling me where to go and what to do. And that was the problem. We'd agreed we were going to have a BDSM relationship. She shouldn't have been acting the same.

I waited until lunchtime to bring it up.

"You could make some quesadillas today," she said as we came inside, sweaty and dirty from our hard work. "There are plenty of veggies to grill, and you can use the goats'-milk cheese we made last week."

I shivered, thinking back to the day we'd made the cheese. It'd been my first time, so I'd struggled to get it right. She'd watched over me, never taking her eyes off me as I heated the milk to just the right temperature. When I successfully filtered it through a cheesecloth, she patted my arm and called me a good girl.

"Yes, Mistress." I watched her carefully and was rewarded by the sight of her lips turning upward. She definitely liked it when I called her that. "Is there anything else you'd like to do after we eat?"

She quirked an eyebrow at me, seeming amused by my question. "Anxious to do something else, are you?"

My face heated. My attempt at subtlety had failed. "I guess I'm wondering when everything's going to start."

"Patience, my sweet Cherry. Everything in due time." She stroked my cheek, her gaze soft and affectionate. "I do enjoy the fact that you're excited."

I let my eyes flutter shut as a throb went through my center. I could've played games with her, made her work to find out how much I wanted her. But that wasn't the type of submissive I aspired to be. I wasn't a brat or a troublemaker. All I wanted was to submit to her, fully and completely. All I'd wanted since I'd met her was to please her.

"I'm more excited than you know, Mistress."

I expected her to drop her hand, to leave me hanging again - but she continued to touch me, and her hand left my skin tingling. She stared into my eyes, and the light gray color of hers shifted and glowed, a million times more complex than I'd ever noticed before.

My core was getting as tight as the night before, maybe even more so because Margo was right in front of me. The way her eyes fluttered to my lips, then back to my eyes, made me think she might be ready to kiss me - finally.

She took a step closer, and I trembled. I was more nervous than I rightfully should've been, considering how badly I'd been wanting this - but then, this was my first kiss with a woman, as well as my first step onto the pathway of kink she intended to lead me down.

"Scared?" she asked, her lips inches from mine, her breath heating my skin.

"No, just..." I inhaled, noticing for the first time how her own spicy scent mingled with the smells of the farm work we'd been doing. "Just ready."

Her head dipped further toward mine, her eyes searching mine for one last confirmation. I was too caught up in my own lust to even give it to her. The pulse between my legs pounded in time with my heart. I couldn't breathe, couldn't even think.

And yet she was still those few inches away, waiting for my consent. I could read the question in her eyes - couldn't she read the answer in mine? Either way, she wanted to hear it from me, and all I wanted was to please her.

I pulled myself together enough to get the words out. "Kiss me, Mistress. Please."

A slight smile curving up her mouth, she brushed her lips against mine. The touch only lasted a millisecond, and it was as light as a butterfly's brief landing. I'd finally gotten what I wanted. I didn't even care if we were dirty and sweaty. What I did care about was that the touch had only left me craving more.

"How was that?" she asked, giving my shoulder a soft squeeze.

"Not enough," I breathed. "Kiss me again."

"Kiss you, who?"

"Mistress." My heart was in my throat, and I would've said whatever it took to get her to do what I asked. "Kiss me again, please. Please."

So she did, the kiss lingering half a second longer than before. It was long enough to taste her minty flavor, to savor the softness of her lips. I shivered at the sensuality of it all, and far too soon, it was over.

"How about that one?" she asked, giving me a devilish smile. "Was that enough for you?"

"Oh, Mistress, I don't think it'll ever be enough." I took a deep breath. "I want one more kiss."

"Just one more, and then you'll make us lunch?"

"Yes, but I want you to make it a good one… if that's all right, Mistress."

"I don't know, sweet Cherry. What makes a good kiss?"

I blushed again, knowing she'd make me spell out every single little thing. "It has to last longer than a second, Mistress. It should probably last a minute or two, actually. There has to be at least a little touching… And it has to involve tongue. Lots of tongue."

"Ah, that's not one kiss. You're talking about a make-out." She smiled again. "Do you want to make out with me, Cherry?"

I nodded meekly.

"Say it. Tell me what you want."

"I want to make out with you," I obediently said – then quickly added the magic word. "Mistress."

A grin took over her face, lighting up her features. "I'd be happy to oblige."

She pulled me close so that her breasts pressed up against mine. The feeling of them – of her – made a coil of heat unspool in my belly. This felt so natural… so damn good. How had I ever thought for one second that I wouldn't want this?

I let my eyes flutter shut as she brought her lips to mine for a third time. We meshed slowly together, then came together with more passion. This time, she was giving me more than just a taste.

Her tongue nudged at the seam of my lips, and I opened eagerly to let her inside. She flicked her tongue under my teeth, and I allowed my own to come up and meet hers. We explored each other, and I found my legs trembling as my heartbeat stuttered. This was everything I'd dreamed of, and it was amazing and magical and utterly overwhelming.

In the end, I was the one to break away. "I can't handle any more."

A worried look came over her face. "Not good?"

"Too good," I breathed.

Her satisfied expression came back. "That's perfect. Ready to make lunch?"

If I could manage to stay upright, I was. "Yes, Mistress."

Eleven

More than anything, I longed to tell someone about the new experiences I was having. Even though Margo and I hadn't gotten to the point of taking off our clothes, every day brought new and bigger thrills. I was on this path now, and there was no turning back.

I couldn't tell Tyler, obviously. I hadn't heard a word from him since our break-up call, and I hoped it'd stay that way. He'd taken me off his social media, and I'd barely blinked when I realized it. I'd moved all of my things out of his place months ago, so that wouldn't be an issue. I never had to see him again.

But I was bursting with excitement, and I couldn't keep it inside. My friends had drifted so far out of touch, they didn't even know I was on this trip. My sister, though, did.

"Julie!" I said on the phone one night after making sure Margo was out of the house. "How's it going? How's your week been?"

"So boring," she groaned. "I swear, every day at work is the exact same. Nothing's changed since the last time I talked to you. I'm tempted to ditch everything and run off to a farm in the middle of nowhere, too."

"You should," I said. "You wouldn't regret it.

It's awesome!"

Julie was a software salesperson. Most of our family was in sales, probably because we were damn good at it. She was two years older than me, and she'd been working at the same company since she'd finished college. It made sense that she was bored. After three years in the same place, I would've been going crazy.

"Really?" she asked. "Farm life's agreeing with you now?"

Right, I hadn't updated her since my first couple of difficult weeks. "It's going a lot better," I told her. "I'm no farmer, but I've definitely gotten used to how things go here. And there's some other stuff going on, too."

My voice had dipped lower at the end of my sentence, and that must have piqued her curiosity. "Like, in a sexy way?"

"Well… umm… yeah. Tyler and I broke up."

"What?" She sounded horrified - they'd always gotten along well, and like everyone else, she'd always thought we were going to get married and spend our future together. "What are you talking about? What happened?"

"The spark wasn't there anymore. But it's not important! I'm honestly not even thinking about him anymore. There's this other person, who just…" I sighed dreamily. "I can't begin to explain."

"But you were together for three years. You

were in love. You can't have moved on that fast."

"I think it ended a while ago. I just hadn't realized it."

"Okay… I'm trying to make sense of everything here." She was thinking aloud like she always did. "You met someone else already… but didn't you say there's no one else out there? Isn't it just you and the farmer?"

"Uh-huh." I waited for her to put two and two together.

"Isn't the farmer… a woman?"

"I told you it was exciting!"

"Just a second." She paused the call, and then her astonished face popped up on my phone screen. "You're dating a woman, Cherry? I'm so confused."

"Join the club." I shrugged playfully. "I have no idea what's going on, but I'm loving every minute of it."

"All right…" She shook her head as if trying to make sense of this. "I'm glad you're having fun."

"So you don't mind or anything?"

"Of course not!"

I'd known she wouldn't. My whole family was progressive and supported equal rights for everyone. Still, it was nice to hear her say it. A tiny part of me had been worried.

"I may or may not have snuck a few girl-kisses during my wild days in college, myself," she added with a wink.

"Oh my God! I never knew that. Was it anyone I know?"

"Um... do you remember Adriana Knutson?"

A memory came to mind of a tall, leggy brunette. "Wow, she was hot!"

Julie chuckled. "Sounds like you are a little gay. I can't believe you just figured this out."

I scoffed. "As if you had any clue, either."

"Anyway, how is it so far?" Her eyes sparkled. "You know, what's it like? Without giving me too much information."

"Hmm... well, not a lot has happened so far. Only one kiss, really - but that kiss was hot." I paused, wondering what qualified as TMI. "It's definitely going to be different, though. This woman, Margo, she likes things pretty kinky. I'm going to be her, um..."

"Her what?" Julie looked totally confused.

"Her submissive," I whispered.

"Oh, shit!" The screen showed her dresser, then her wall - she must've dropped her phone. "TMI, little sis! TMI!"

"Sorry!" I laughed. "You said you wanted to know!"

"All right, well, have fun and be safe."

"Oh, I plan to."

I'd been dreading telling anyone about my break-up because I thought they'd assume I was heartbroken and treat me like a fragile flower. Julie had been more interested in hearing about Margo, which was perfect because she was all I wanted to talk about.

Hopefully things would go just as well when I updated my mother. "What do you think Mom would think of this whole thing?" I asked.

"You can tell her you're dating a woman, and she won't care." Julie's lips twitched like she was fighting a giggle. "I suspect she'd have a similar reaction as me about the rest of it, though."

"The rest of it? Is that what we're going to call it?"

"No, because we're never going to speak of it again."

When we hung up, I was still laughing.

I felt lighter now that I'd spoken to my sister. Even if certain topics were off-limits, she knew what was going on and she was happy for me.

I headed downstairs, where Margo was lounging on the couch, a book in hand. She glanced over at me, quirking an eyebrow. Her oversized flannel shirt had one more button undone than usual, and the peek of skin at her chest made my eyes want to stray there.

But she must've heard everything. I tensed up, suddenly self-conscious. "How long have you been in here?"

"Long enough." She sat up with a cocky grin. "You had a good chat with your friend, huh?"

"My sister," I mumbled. "Yeah."

"No wonder she didn't want to hear about it."

I looked away. "Usually we tell each other everything."

"Don't worry about that. Come here." She gestured at me to sit beside her, and when I did, she placed her arm around my shoulders. My heart beat faster as she continued to speak. "You were a good girl today, my sweet Cherry. I think it's time to get you ready for the next step."

My breath went shallow. "Just get me ready?" I asked in a low voice. "Not actually take the next step?"

"Just get you ready," she confirmed.

"What does that mean?" I could barely think when she was touching me like this.

Turning toward me, she brushed my hair back from my face and brought her lips to mine. She hadn't kissed me again since the first time, and I'd been too terrified to ask - so this embrace took away my last bit of ability to think. I melted into her arms, and she left me breathless when she eventually pulled away.

"You'll see," she said - as calm as ever, but there

was a darkness in her eyes that betrayed her desire for me. "Come with me."

I followed her to her room, my excitement and fear both rising with every step. I'd never been behind this door before, and going inside was going to be a new layer of intimacy.

"Don't look so scared," she said, placing a hand on the small of my back. "I don't have a dungeon or a playroom. I'm not that fancy."

The room was similar to mine, except it had larger windows that would've let plenty of light in during the day. The walls were bare clay, with a single painting above the headboard of the bed – a woman seated on the floor, pictured from behind. Her wrists were chained together with thick silver cuffs.

My heart pounded in my throat. Was that what Margo wanted to do to me? Quickly, I looked away. The bed looked like mine, which made me a little more comfortable. It had the same kind of ratty plaid blanket, and I was pretty sure the thin mattress was the same, too.

"Although the bedposts do come in handy," she said.

She had a small bookshelf in here, too, and I advanced toward it as if drawn by a magnet. I read over the titles and chuckled softly, even as my center throbbed. I could see why she kept these ones up here. They were along the same lines as her BDSM collection below, but far more explicit. They had titles like Making Your Sub

Scream for More and The Complete Guide to Japanese Rope Bondage.

I pulled my eyes downward, only to have them pop out once more. Rather than books, the lower part of her bookshelf contained a variety of items - some I recognized, some I didn't. There was a black leather whip with metal studs on the handle, a huge alien-looking object I thought was called a Hitachi magic wand, a studded black harness with an uncomfortably realistic-looking dildo poking through, and more.

"What do you think?" Margo's voice came from behind me, curious yet still self-assured.

I glanced back at her nervously. "You're really into this stuff."

"I didn't think that would be a surprise." She stood behind me, letting her arms encircle my waist as she looked over her toys with me. "Tell me, what here interests you the most?"

My throat went dry. Everything here seemed like it was from a completely different world. It was hard to believe that my light-hearted conversation with Julie had only happened a few minutes ago. Entering this room was like stepping into another dimension.

"Umm..." I knew the answer, I was just too shy to say it. "Maybe..."

"Point to it, Cherry."

My hand moved upward of its own accord, and my finger jutted toward the huge strap-on dildo.

"This one, Mistress." My voice was only a whisper.

"You want me to fuck you?" Her breath was on my ear, and yet goosebumps rose all over my body.

"Yes, Mistress."

"And what about the other way around?" She squeezed my waist slightly, hinting at all the other ways she wanted to overpower me. "Would you like to use it on me, too?"

I looked at her sharply. "Wouldn't that defeat the whole point?"

"How so?"

I licked my lips, considering. It seemed obvious to me, but she was acting like it was completely not obvious. "Wouldn't that mean I was dominating you? Wouldn't I be taking control?"

She raised an eyebrow, looking thoroughly amused. "So the man is always in control, is he? Always dominant? Has your partner dominated you every time you've ever had sex?"

"Well... no."

"Think about it, Cherry. There are plenty of ways you could use that while I'd still be in charge." Her eyes glittered at me meaningfully.

I tried to imagine what she meant. I pictured myself chained up, lying on my back, the toy jutting up from between my legs. Margo could straddle me, ease her way onto the dildo... She could lower herself slowly, pressing a hand over my mouth or her fingers between my lips. I'd watch her wetness glide over the toy, watch her breasts heave as she rode me. I'd want to touch her so desperately, but with my hands restrained, I'd be completely helpless.

"Okay." I tried - and failed - to bring my heavy breathing back to normal. "I think I see what you mean."

"Good," she said. "We'll save that idea for later."

Taking my hand, she led me toward her bathroom. Now, this room was completely different from mine. Where mine was small and cramped, hers was expansive, even luxurious. A wide window looked out on the sunset, and a large bathtub with claw feet was the focus point of the room.

"This is amazing," I said. "I had no idea."

"Of course you didn't." She moved past me and plugged the tub, then perched on the side and turned both handles of the tap until the water flowed. "How do you like your water, my sweet sub? Warm or hot?"

My heart stuttered. "Are we going to take a bath together?"

"Not quite." She gazed up at me, smiling with satisfaction. "I like my women clean. And... hairless."

So it would just be me in the tub? I was fine with

that. If anything, it was a bit anticlimactic. The way she was acting, I'd been sure she was going to touch me more or do something with me. I was so, so tired of waiting.

"I'll be the one bathing you, of course." Her smile darkened. "And shaving you."

My nipples hardened and grazed against the fabric of my shirt. So I was supposed to be naked in the tub, dripping wet and soaped-up, while she stayed fully dressed? "That sounds rather unfair. Why don't I get to bathe you?"

Her lips set in a firm line. "Remember who you're speaking to."

I dropped my eyes. "Yes, Mistress."

"If you truly object, you can always use your safe word. Do you remember what it is?"

I nodded. "'Red light.' And if I want to slow down but not stop, I'll say 'yellow light.'"

"Good. Do you want to use either one now?"

I considered it. I really wasn't sure about the idea of being in the bath without her – but I didn't truly object to it, either. If she was keen to do this, I'd let her try it. Maybe I'd like it more than I thought… especially if she was leading up to something sexual. If I stopped things now, we'd never get there – and I was damn near desperate to.

"No," I said. "We can try."

Her smile now reminded me of the Cheshire cat.

If I'd ever been afraid she wasn't truly into this, that doubt was gone now. That smile said this woman wanted me naked and dripping as soon as humanly possible.

Still, she restrained herself as she calmly dipped a finger in the water. "Feels good to me," she murmured. "Want to check?"

"I trust you."

The bathtub was nearly full, so I stripped off my shirt. It was one of the ones I'd bought for farming, although at this point it was as beat-up and bedraggled as any of Margo's clothes. I had a sports bra underneath, the kind that compressed everything and minimized my chest. I would've worn something sexier if I'd known we'd be doing this.

Margo still took a sharp intake of breath when she saw it. "That looks lovely," she said, her eyes ever-so-slightly wider than before. "But it's not going in the bath with you. Take it off."

I obeyed, pulling the bra over my head and covering myself with one arm as I laid it on the floor. It was silly of me to be self-conscious at this point, but my natural modesty wouldn't allow me to flaunt myself around - especially not when she was fully dressed.

She edged forward on the side of the tub as if drawn forward by my presence. "Drop the arm," she whispered.

Slowly, cautiously, I did as she said. The force of

her stare heated me where it touched my skin, just like her fingers always did. "And now what?" I asked, trying to stop trembling. "Mistress?"

"The pants." She nearly hissed out the words. "On the floor. No covering yourself."

I was sure she could see how much I was shaking as I stripped them off. After dropping them to the ground, I stood tall and hooked my thumbs through my panties, waiting for her to tell me to take them off as well.

She was quiet for a long moment, simply staring at me, studying my body. My face grew hotter from her scrutiny, even as my nipples pebbled. Looking at her right now was too much. I gazed at the bathwater instead.

"Panties off," she finally said.

I eased the pink cotton over my hips and down my thighs. I could feel Margo's tension - or was that my own? The room was getting warmer, or else that was in my head, too.

She moved forward and ran a finger across the dark blonde curls below my waistline. "We'll take care of that."

"How can you live on a farm but expect your women to be shaved?" I normally kept myself bare - I hadn't thought it necessary in this environment.

"Just a preference." She gave a slow, languorous shrug. "It's a visual sign - a reminder that you're mine. Do you want to use your safe word?"

Picturing her smoothing shaving cream across my mound, I shivered. "No. I'm up for it."

"Good girl." She stood up and turned off the water. "I like that you're always ready to try something new."

She took a bath bomb from the counter and tossed it into the tub. The water immediately began to turn different shades of violet.

Slightly chilly without my clothes, I anticipated the heat would feel nice. Once Margo gestured at me to get in, I tried - and promptly shrieked. The water was practically boiling!

Margo patted my arm. "Ease your way in. Take it a little at a time. You'll be glad you did."

In any other situation, I would've trusted her, but that water was going to scald my skin off!

"You only put a toe in," she said patiently. "Try again. Once you're in, you'll acclimatize."

I tried to ignore how strange it felt to be a grown woman with another grown woman instructing me on how to take a bath. As awkward as this was, there was something thrilling about it, too. And surely the heat would be better than the chill of the air, once I got used to it.

I dipped my toe in again, and then the rest of my foot. I took a deep breath as the heat overwhelmed my nervous system. Once I'd recovered slightly, I plunged that foot to the bottom and stepped the other foot in. Squeezing my eyes shut and hugging myself tightly, I lowered myself to the floor of the tub.

"Beautiful." Margo's voice came from above me. "Very good, my sweet Cherry. You already know how to push through the pain, especially when you know there will be a reward on the other side."

I let my eyes flutter open. The bath was already starting to feel more comfortable. Once the heat stopped stinging, it'd actually be enjoyable. I luxuriated across the tub and poked a finger into the purple bubbles.

"I knew you could do it," Margo said approvingly. Perching on the side of the tub again, she rolled up her sleeves. Once the flannel cuffs hung loosely around her slim forearms, she removed her watch as well. "Would you like me to clean you, Cherry?"

My breath came faster. "Yes, Mistress." I nodded for emphasis.

She pulled herself closer, leaning over me. She caressed my cheek for a brief moment, then dipped her hand into the water, scooping up some suds. She rubbed them over my neck, massaging me as she scrubbed me. I arched up, hoping she'd move on to my breasts next.

Instead, she picked up my right arm and gave it the same treatment, kneading with her fingers and thumbs as she rubbed the bubbles all over me. The ache between my legs was growing, and my breasts and nipples begged to be touched.

Somehow, I had a feeling Margo wouldn't be fulfilling my needs anytime soon. If there was one thing I'd learned about her, it was that she loved to tease me.

All I could do was sit back and enjoy the tease. And it was enjoyable - the slide of her hands along my wet skin, her palms pushing into the flesh, her slim fingers dancing. I was even starting to like how she kept me aroused for so long and never followed through. I liked it because I knew she would follow through in her own good time - and that when she did, it'd be magnificent.

As she finished my left arm, I arched my back, pushing my breasts up. The peaks of my nipples broke the surface of the water, rising up between violet suds.

She hummed in appreciation. "Did you want something, my sweet Cherry?"

"Only for you to touch me, Mistress."

"I'm getting there."

Ignoring my plea, she worked her way across the top of my breastbone, and then down the center of my chest. She paid no attention to my breasts themselves, as if their presence didn't even affect her - although I could see her pupils dilate every time she glanced at them.

When her hands found my stomach, she shifted slightly to be able to reach me better. She grazed her fingers over me, equal parts cleaning and caressing. I bit my lip, conscious of her proximity to my core. The closer she came, the hotter I got. If and when she ever touched me there, I'd probably explode entirely.

She moved down to my hips, then my thighs. I sat quietly, struggling to breathe as she made her way down each leg in turn. Not an inch of my body would go unscrubbed, it seemed, and once she was done with my feet, I'd find out how she intended to deal with my more private areas.

"Turn over." She let the left foot go.

I whipped my head at her. "What do you mean?"

"Get on your front, sweet Cherry. I need to clean your back."

I lay down as best as I could. Once she was done with my back, though, she pulled my hips upward, silently signalling me to get on my knees.

"What…"

"I need to clean all of you."

Her soapy fingers slipped into my crack for a brief second. As soon as I understood what she was doing, it was over.

"That's all," she said, pushing me to turn over.

"Now for the fun part."

I sucked in a breath. So she was going to go over all the parts she'd avoided before? My suspicion was confirmed as her hands moved over my breasts, spreading violet bubbles over them as she cupped them.

My nipples pressed against her palms, begging for her attention. When she flicked her thumbs over them, I couldn't help myself. I moaned.

Every time she moved her fingers across the tight pink buds, sparks of bliss flew through my core. And she only kept going. My nipples were harder than they'd ever been, and the ache in my center was becoming unbearable.

Finally she slid down the tub, and I let my breasts sink beneath the surface of the water. "Whenever you'd like to unplug the drain, go ahead," she told me. "Then I'll shave you."

It was an impossible choice. The hot water, which had been so painful at first, had become a source of joy. And yet I wanted her hands on me just as badly as I wanted to continue to soak.

My sex drive won out over my need to stay in the heat. The sooner she shaved me, the sooner she might touch me - or do more than that. I unplugged the drain and watched the sudsy water flow out.

Some of the purple bubbles lingered on me when the tub had emptied. It didn't matter - I expected I'd need to shower after Margo shaved me. After she shaved me! I'd accepted so quickly that this bizarrely intimate act was going to happen.

That it was about to happen. She took a can of shaving cream from the counter, along with an old-fashioned straight razor. My center tingled, and I couldn't help but push my legs together where I stood in the tub. There was no way I'd be able to keep her from seeing my wetness, but I was sure going to try.

She gazed at the fine smattering of pubic hair, slowly shaking her head. "No, it simply won't do," she said to herself.

Coming closer to me, she pressed her fingers to my pubic mound, pulling my skin taut. My legs shook, and blood rushed to my spot. No one had ever touched me like this before touching me there immediately afterward - and yet Margo clearly had no intention of doing so. She squirted shaving cream onto her fingers and spread it across the top inch of hair.

Oh God, she was going to do this as slowly, as torturously as she'd cleaned the rest of my body. My suspicion came true as she picked up the razor. Neatly, carefully, she brought it over that one foamed-up inch, one razor-width at a time until she'd crossed my mound - and then she spread the cream over the next inch and repeated the process.

Heat spread through my face and chest, and I let out a low groan. This was going to take hours -

or at least it was going to feel that way. For something that should've been humiliating, it was uncomfortably arousing. I tried to ignore the desire pooling in my core.

"How are you feeling, sweet Cherry?" Margo asked. "It's not too much for you, is it?"

"Not at all." The words came out in a breath. "I… Please keep going."

Her nimble fingers brought the razor over the foam, picking up brown curls as it passed. The skin she laid bare was more sensitive now that it was wet and exposed, and it tingled as cool air passed over it.

I looked away as Margo's hands did their work. She was getting closer to my center now, and I had no idea what was going to happen. If her fingers even brushed over my clit, I might fall head-over-heels into orgasm. A cool breeze could've sent me over the edge at the moment.

She tugged one of my lower lips away from the other folds, expertly avoiding touching anything else. As I fought a full-body shudder, she smoothed cream over both sides of the labium.

"Be careful, sweet Cherry," she said, looking up at me with amusement. "Shiver like that, and I might cut you by accident."

"I'll try to stop." My voice was choked.

She ran the razor along the sensitive flesh, and the shave was like a caress. To keep myself from moaning, I held my breath until she finished.

Once she let go, I let it all out in a sigh – and then she took the other lip into her hand. My eyes squeezed shut, and I caught my breath again. If she'd just move her hands one inch to the side, she'd be exactly where I needed her. If she'd just give me one little touch, even a graze of her fingers…

"All done!" she said cheerily. "Do you want to take a look?"

I gave her a half-nod and stepped out of the tub, still dripping as I stood in front of the mirror. My bald pussy with bits of foam still clinging to it was nothing new – I'd shaved many times before. The part that was different was Margo standing beside me, fully dressed while I was completely naked, her eyes sweeping up and down my reflection with a look of self-satisfaction.

Her approval was the one thing I craved above all else, and right now, I had it.

"Shower off." Her voice was ever-so-slightly hoarse. "Then you can go back to your room."

"And you'll join me there?" I asked hopefully.

"Nice try, my dear." She put her hands on my waist, holding me from behind as she pressed her lips to the side of my neck. "This is all you're getting for tonight. We'll talk more tomorrow."

TWELVE

The day after Margo shaved me, I tried to go about my daily duties and milk Harmony as if nothing had happened. I could feel the bareness of my skin, though, and even the slight itch of the hair growing back made my little bud harden. I'd satisfied myself last night - many times, and thoroughly - but it couldn't compare to the real thing. I needed Margo desperately. I had to trust she'd let me have her soon.

Sitting on my usual stool, I tugged and squeezed Harmony's teat like usual. Less milk was coming out, though. I was sure I wasn't doing it any differently than usual - and I'd become a real pro at it over the past six weeks - so what was the deal?

I kept trying until Margo came into the barn. "What's taking you so long?"

"About time you showed up. I'm getting less milk today." I gestured at the half-empty bucket.

She nodded to me to get off the stool, then took my place. I watched over her shoulder, equal parts curious and nervous. If she could get more milk out of Harmony, that'd mean I'd failed somehow. But I'd done everything the exact same as usual!

She coaxed a few more trickles out of the goat,

who bleated despondently with her last squeezes. "Well, she's drying up," Margo said, standing up. "Seems a little early, but I suppose it has been almost ten months since she gave birth."

"Oh… so we can't milk her much longer?" I remembered the lecture she'd given me early on about how precious Harmony's milk was. "What happens now?"

"We'll keep her until the feed we give her is worth more than the amount of milk that we get. Should be a week or two more." She strode out of the barn and into the sunlight. "Then we'll slaughter her."

My eyes nearly popped out of my head. "Slaughter Harmony?"

She turned to look back at me with a perplexed smile. "Yes, what did you think was going to happen? I told you she wasn't going to have any more kids."

"I know, but…" The goat was so cute, with her big brown eyes and her soft, twitching ears. I'd gotten fond of her from milking her. I didn't even mind going to third base with her every morning. "I guess I thought you'd keep her."

"She's not a pet, Cherry." She brushed a hand over my arm as we walked toward the fields. "My little city girl… Harmony had to earn her keep. If she can't give milk anymore, she has to do that in another way."

I stopped short. "You can't mean… You're not going to…"

Margo stopped, too, raising her eyebrows at me. "Eat her? Yes, my dear. Where do you think meat comes from?"

"From the store," I said in a small voice, picturing the sanitized flesh in shrink-wrapped packages. I never normally associated it with the actual animals it came from. "Or the restaurant."

"This is the real world, my sweet Cherry. The food chain - eat or be eaten."

Except Harmony would never eat me. She was a kind soul, a herbivore. She was my friend.

I reminded myself of the story Margo had told me - the woman she thought was the love of her life, who turned out to be too much of a city girl for them to stay together. I didn't want to be like Jasmine. Even if this was only a casual relationship, I couldn't let her see how much of a city girl I really was. I had to steel myself and accept that Harmony - my sweet baby - had to die.

I could deal with it. Margo was right - this was no different from the meat I ate every day. I was being silly and sentimental because I had a particular bond with this animal. But that was all Harmony was, an animal. They were here for us to eat. Right?

Margo looked back at me, and the dismay remaining on my face must have been visible.

"This will be more ethical than the meat you buy from the grocery store," she said. "You know Harmony's had a good life, and that she'll be slaughtered in a humane way. The things they do to animals on factory farms, in contrast, are horrifying."

"That's true," I murmured, trying to convince myself I believed her.

"And no part of her body will go to waste," she went on. "I'll use her skin for – "

"Okay!" I waved a hand, feeling sick. "I don't need to hear the details!"

We reached the field, and she handed me a shovel. "No problem."

I let my feelings fester as we worked for the rest of the morning. I didn't bring up the subject of Harmony while we ate lunch – but before we got back to work in the afternoon, I snuck back into the barn to run the goat's soft fur through my fingers and gaze into her big brown eyes. I hand-fed her a bit of hay, too. If she only had a week or two left to live, I was going to make them as pleasant as possible. Still, my heart clenched in my chest as I walked out of the barn.

The afternoon passed without incident – unless my despair when I thought about Harmony counted as an incident. When we finished up for the day, we showered off the filth of the farm as usual. I ran my fingers along my bare mound in the shower, wondering when Margo would take the next step. The shaving was to get me ready for that, wasn't it?

When I emerged from the shower, still in my towel, I found Margo seated on my bed. "You seem upset today," she said, gazing at me steadily. "Come here and let me make it better."

As much as I was upset, my body responded to the suggestion just as much as it would've any other day. Heat instantly rose, and wetness built between my thighs. "Make it up to me how?" I asked softly.

Rather than telling me, she gestured at me to lie down. I got on my front, and she unwrapped the towel down to my waist. Her hands settled onto my shoulders, and she rubbed and kneaded the way she had the night before, in the bath.

I pressed my face into the pillow, luxuriating in the feel of her hands on my body. Surely tonight would be the night we went all the way. Blood rushed to my center as her massage built up my desire. The more she touched and pressed me, the more I wanted her hands somewhere else.

"Mistress," I started hesitantly. "Could you... Would you..."

She brushed the hair off the back of my neck, then caressed my nape lovingly. "Would I what, sweet Cherry?"

"Touch..." My breath was coming in shallow gasps. "Touch me..."

"But I am touching you." She was evil.

I hated having to spell out what I wanted. "Not there." I rolled over, immediately exposing my breasts. The towel fell open, leaving my lower half bare, too – including my freshly-shaved pussy. "Here." I grabbed her hand and brought it to my wetness, and the first brush of her fingers brought a sharp intake of breath through my lips.

She was affected, too. Her voice was hoarse when she spoke again. "You want me to rub your clit? Make little circles on it?" She did what she was saying as she asked about it.

"Yes-s-s," I hissed. "All of the above."

"Mmm… I can do that." She kept touching me. "Soft? Or hard?"

"However you want to, Mistress. Do what you want with me."

That must've been the right answer. The desire on her face intensified, and she shifted over to have easier access to me.

"How about this?" she asked, bringing her fingers down to my lower lips. "Do you want me to play with your pussy? Tease your entrance? Or maybe everything at once?"

That sounded good… but there was something even more urgent. "I want you to go inside."

A smile curved up her lips as she pushed her finger in to the knuckle. My walls spasmed around her, and I choked out a gasp. "How's that, sweet Cherry?"

"More," I breathed. "Give me… more…"

She pushed her finger the rest of the way inside, and my breath was knocked out of my throat. How did this feel so - damn - good? Was it because she'd been teasing me and denying me for weeks leading up to this? Or was this just how it would be between me and her?

Instead of thrusting in and out of me like I expected, she curled her finger slightly to hit a spot on my inner wall. My eyes rolled back in my head, and my hips jumped up to meet her. I couldn't restrain my desire. The tiny movements of her finger were making me go out of control.

"Is that enough for you, my dear?" she asked, leaning over me so she could press a kiss to my quivering stomach. "Or would you like my tongue on you, too?"

I didn't hesitate for a second. "Yes. Yes, yes, yes." I nodded enthusiastically even as I gyrated. "Please, Mistress, give me your tongue."

Her pupils dilated as she lowered herself slowly toward my center. She was dragging this out, moving only an inch at a time. Even with her finger inside me, she was still finding new ways to torture me.

She hovered just above my mound, her breath heating the area she'd shaved yesterday. "Are you sure you want it?" she asked coyly. "I'm not quite sure how you feel."

Oh, I hated her. Hated her with a burning passion. I thrust my hips up as if trying to push my clit against her lips, but she deftly moved away. "Tell me, sweet Cherry."

"I'm very sure," I panted. "I don't just want it. I need it. Lick me, Mistress. Go down on me. Please."

Her smirk gave away how satisfied she was with herself. "Well, since you asked nicely."

Keeping her finger inside me, she brushed her tongue briefly over my swollen nub. I cried out and thrashed, overcome by the power of the sensation. As she grazed over it a second time, my hips moved with her tongue as if I could keep her from taking it away.

I couldn't, of course. If she wanted to torture me, my resistance would be futile. Thankfully, the time for torture appeared to finally - finally - be over. She stayed between my legs, drawing her tongue up and down in languorous strokes as her finger come-hithered inside me.

The sensations washing over me were too strong to suppress. My climax was building - so soon, sooner than it ever had with anyone else, and yet I wasn't surprised in the slightest. I let go of whatever remained of my inhibitions as Margo's tongue swirled faster and harder. Before I knew what was happening, the world around me burst into an explosion of white light.

My hips pushed against her tongue in a silent plea. I could feel her hands on my hips, holding me in place as I spasmed. Quickly, expertly, she brought me to a second orgasm - and then a third.

When I couldn't come anymore, I squirmed away. I fell against the pillow, thoroughly exhausted.

She came up beside me, wrapping her arms around my back. Infuriatingly, she was still fully clothed.

"Have you forgiven me for Harmony yet, sweet Cherry?"

A bitter taste rose in my mouth. I'd almost forgotten.

No, I hadn't forgiven her. And I doubted I ever would.

THIRTEEN

Every day, Harmony's bucket was a little less full. The end of her milk days was nearing, and yet I felt no more comfortable with the idea of slaughtering her. There was no way I'd ever be able to eat the flesh of my friend.

I waited until after dessert one night to bring up the suggestion I'd come up with. Margo sat with her hands on her stomach, her eyes closed, a smudge of ice cream on the corner of her mouth.

I bent in to lick it off her, shocked by my own boldness as I did. She opened her eyes and smiled at me, and I decided it was okay to be bold for once.

"I had an idea," I said. "What if you don't kill Harmony?"

Her eyebrows shot up. "We've been over this."

"No, let me finish. I mean, I'm leaving in a little over a month." The end date for my farm journey was sneaking up way too fast. Every time I thought about going back to "real life," I felt funny inside. "You could wait until then to do it. If feeding her is a burden, I'll pay for her food. She'll be company for me until I leave."

She kept her eyebrows high on her forehead. "Like a pet, Cherry?"

"Well… kind of." I coughed. "But she'll be my pet. And it'll be temporary. I'm not telling you what to do when I'm gone." She'd probably start dating other women, playing with other subs, the moment I left. The idea shouldn't have bothered me as much as it did.

"I don't know about this," she said. "The food chain is part of life on a farm. I think not slaughtering her would take away from your experience here."

"And what if it does? It's my experience to do what I want with." I bit my lip. "I care about Harmony. Don't do anything until I'm gone. Please…. Mistress."

Her expression immediately softened - yet she remained resolute. "This is Harmony's time. It's how the circle of life works, from birth to death. This time will come for all of us, even you."

She didn't know how close I'd already come. "But it's you who's deciding in this case," I said. "You could change your mind. You could keep her until I leave." Or forever.

"This is life on a farm, my dear. If you can't handle it, then…"

I stared at her, horrified. Did she mean I should leave? Even though we were sleeping together?

Of course she meant that. I couldn't be fooled by her sweetness and all the pet names she called me. What we had was casual, meaningless. She didn't care about me. She'd choose killing a goat over me staying.

"Fine," I mumbled, looking down. "I can handle it."

She gazed at me with sympathy - whether it was genuine or fake, I didn't know right now. "You'll be okay, I'm sure of it. You eat meat, you're not a vegan or anything."

"No, I only care about Harmony." Although I couldn't see myself eating goat again anytime soon. Actually, going vegan didn't sound like such a bad idea.

"All right, my dear. Let's do some cleaning. I'm planning to slaughter her on Saturday, then have some neighbors over for a goat roast on Sunday."

My stomach turned, even as I got up and grabbed the broom. I wasn't going to be able to think about anything but Harmony until this whole thing was over. And maybe not even then.

I might not even be able to get turned on or to be intimate with Margo. All I could see was her coldness toward Harmony - and toward me.

Once the silence in the room became oppressive, I decided to change the subject. "What are your neighbors like?" I asked. "Are they like you?"

"You mean dominants?" She stood in front of the sink, washing the dishes.

I couldn't help a snort. "I mean, you know...

hippies, feminists, lesbians."

"Some are. Some aren't." She shrugged. "It's a bit of a mix around here. There are those who were born into this life - the old-school farmers - and those who chose it willingly - the off-the-grid granola types. Then there are those who fit both descriptions, like me."

"The old-school farmers and granola types get along?"

She shrugged. "Well enough. There's some conflict when we get to discussing farming methods, but we all help each other out when needed. When someone needs to borrow a tractor, there are ten people willing to lend one. And we share with each other, like when we have an exceptional harvest or a tasty cut of meat."

My poor Harmony.

"Those of us who've been doing this for a long time give the newbies lots of advice," she went on. "Some of them give up and move back to the city anyway. Those who stick around are as accepted as anybody else."

I put the broom aside and reached for the mop and bucket. "What are your plans for Sunday night?"

"Mostly eating and drinking a lot. Ed and his husband Lewis will bring some home-brewed wine and beer - a lot of the neighbors try, but those two are absolute pros at it. Sandra will bring some of her amazing persimmon chutney, you have to try it. My mouth is watering just thinking about it."

"It sounds good." And I loved how passionate Margo got when she talked about food. I just wished that didn't include goat.

"Sandra's my sister, by the way."

"Oh!" She'd never mentioned any specific family members before. It was hard to imagine her as a sister or a daughter. To me, she seemed like she must've fallen to earth fully formed. "Is she older or younger?"

"Three years older. She lives half an hour away on her own farm, so I see her more often than my parents."

"Where are they now?"

"They retired from farming here a few years ago," she said. "Then they bought some land in Costa Rica. They live there now, growing food and learning Spanish, trying to set up the same kind of conscious community they had here."

"Wow."

She finished washing the dishes and grabbed a cloth to dry them. "What kind of relationships do you have in your life?" she asked. "Do you want to talk about your ex-boyfriend?"

"Not particularly." I cringed at the mention. "But I will if you want to hear about him. You must be curious."

"Not particularly." She chuckled. "It must not have been a strong connection if you were willing to leave him so suddenly."

"It was strong at one point, but… we went through a lot." I bit my lip. I'd never had to dance around talking about my health issues. Back home, they were all anyone could think about. "I guess we grew apart without realizing it. Then I quit my job and came here, and I changed even more."

"What inspired you to quit your job? I don't think I ever asked you."

"I just…"

I was happy to be alive - that was the real answer. But I couldn't open up to Margo about all of that.

It felt strange to not tell her, especially when she'd openly asked me about it earlier. But I couldn't. She'd look at me differently. She'd never want to sleep with me. She'd treat me like I was some fragile object, and I wasn't. I was as healthy as I'd ever been - all of that was in the past.

"I felt like I needed to," I finally said. "I wasn't fulfilled. I felt like I'd gotten as good at car sales as I was going to, and it wasn't doing anything for me. The money was good, but what was the point of it all? To make the car manufacturers richer? To bring more pollution onto this planet?" I sighed. "I wanted to find more meaning in my life."

"So you decided to come here." She put the last dry dish in the cupboard and came over to me, taking the mop out from between us.

"Yes."

"I'm glad you did." She gazed down at me affectionately.

Fuck, my heart hurt. I wanted to be mad at her for the whole Harmony thing. I wanted to not care how much she cared about me.

Moments like this, it felt like she did care. And I liked that… a little too much.

This was casual. No strings attached. She'd never go for a city girl, and I most definitely was one.

I couldn't be like her neighbors, who'd gotten accepted into the farming community. I didn't want to live out here permanently. My life, my real life, was back at home.

Not that she'd ever want me to move out here. The fact that we'd had sex – incredible sex – didn't mean this was anything more than a fling.

She stroked my face, and I melted inside. There was no way I could stay mad at her. As her face approached mine, I turned to absolute mush.

Our lips met, and I let my arms fall around her shoulders as I pressed my body to hers. Our breasts pressing together, her fragrant Margo scent in my nose…

Harmony or no Harmony, how could I ever say

no to this woman?

I hummed in bliss, the bliss of her touch and her kiss. When we were together like this, nothing else mattered. The world outside us faded away more with every moment that we embraced. There was no house, no farm, no animals - only her lips pressing gently against mine, her tongue sliding sweetly into my mouth.

No words needed to be said - we both knew we were going to take this upstairs. She left me panting, breathless, when she broke away from the kiss, and her hand on my lower back, guiding me, cut my breath in a whole new way.

My heartbeat sped up as we ascended the stairs. My nerves were lit up, my body aflame. If this was anything like the last time, she'd make me come apart and then put me all the way back together again.

At some point, I hoped she'd give me the chance to let me do the same to her.

In her room, we kissed again, our passion even hotter now that we were in such close proximity to the bed. Her curves were sensually soft under my hands, and her lips and tongue were even more tender.

"What would you like today, my dear, sweet Cherry?" she asked, her eyes half-lidded, her voice practically a purr.

"Something like last time." My hands slid under the hem of her flannel shirt and pushed far enough up to feel the warm skin of her stomach. "Except... I'd like to do all of that to you, too."

"To who?"

"To you, Mistress."

"Good." She pushed my hands back down, her eyes seductive yet firm. "But not today, my sweet. Not yet."

"Today is just about me?"

"Mm-hmm." She drew her fingernails down my neck and into the neckline of my top. If she went much further, she'd encounter my bra cups – and my nipples pebbled at the thought. "I need to make you feel better about certain things, after all."

My heart sank. I could've done without the reminder. "Okay," I murmured. "In that case, could we maybe..."

"Maybe what, sweet Cherry?"

"Maybe... get a little kinkier?" I could barely get the words out. As it stood, they were only a whisper.

Her eyes flashed with amusement. "What kind of kinkier?" She spun me around to look at the bookshelf where she kept all her kinky equipment. "Tell me what you want."

"Maybe..." My fingers quivering, I pointed at a set of black leather cuffs with straps attached. "And..." The strip of black satin that sat beside it.

"I said tell me, Cherry."

I licked my suddenly dry lips, embarrassed at how I'd messed up. "I want that, Mistress." Again, I pointed. "I'm not sure exactly what it's called... I think they're cuffs, or maybe handcuffs."

"Those are under-bed restraints," she told me, still holding me from behind, her breasts pressed against my back. "The long straps go under the bed to hold you immobilized from each side. The specific parts that will hold your wrists are cuffs, yes."

"Ah..." A blaze of heat went through me. "I want all of that. And this..." I fingered the silky fabric. "I think it's supposed to be used as a blindfold."

"That's correct, my dear." Picking up the items in question, she led me over to the bed. "Take off your clothes for me and lie down on your back."

I did as she said, less nervous about exposing myself this time. I still wanted to see her without her clothes, but I was getting used to being naked while she was dressed. I'd taken care to maintain her shaving work, and she nodded approvingly when she saw that.

"I'm going to restrain your hands, then your legs," she said. "Remember your safe word, okay?"

"Yes, Mistress." I already knew I wouldn't have

to use it.

She slid a cuff over one wrist, and I toyed with it while she ran the strap under the bed. Once she came up, she cuffed my other wrist and went down to my feet. I tugged at the restraints, testing how secure they were.

Seeing me when she came up, she raised an eyebrow. "I didn't tell you to move."

My stomach dropped. "I'm sorry, Mistress." How badly had I fucked up? Would she be angry enough to end the scene?

"On a scale from one to ten, what you just did ranks at a two," she told me, gazing down at my nude body appreciatively. "I'm going to punish you anyway."

My breath caught in my throat.

"You told me you wanted to get kinkier," she reminded me.

I turned my head to the side, shallow pants coming through my lips. She'd bound my legs so far apart that cool air gusted against my pussy, making me wetter by the second. "So what are you going to do?"

"Telling you would ruin the fun." She ran the blindfold across her palm, her expression implacably calm. "In fact, you're not going to see it coming."

I suppressed a low groan as wetness dripped down my inner thigh. How was I this turned on? I was allowing her control of not only my body, but also my senses – I'd never guessed this would be so hot.

I shivered as her fingers made contact with my forehead. Within seconds, the blindfold was firmly fastened around my eyes and my field of vision was blocked completely.

"Can you see anything, sweet Cherry?"

"No."

"Nothing at all? Don't lie to me now."

I sucked in a breath. "Only a bit of light at the bottom… I might be able to see you moving around."

She adjusted the blindfold, making me shiver again. "How is it now?"

"Perfect." The word came out husky.

Blind to the world, I couldn't say for sure what she was doing. I could take a pretty good guess that those were her fingertips sweeping down the cleft between my breasts, then across my belly and over my mound.

I struggled to breathe as she kept up her light grazes. Was this the punishment? Because as incredible as it felt, the sheer amount of teasing could've made it a negative thing.

Something brushed against my left nipple – still just her fingers, I thought. I was convinced that was true when she squeezed slightly. Another, less gentle tweak, and I let out a yelp.

"I thought you weren't a sadist," I breathed.

"Are you in pain?"

"No, I just..." I grimaced as she tweaked again – and yet I couldn't deny the fresh shot of desire that went straight to my core. "Never mind. I – I like it."

She continued her gentle assault, playing with one nipple until the pleasure verged on pain, and then switching to the other while the first recovered. She managed it so expertly, I wondered how she knew when I was at my edge. Were all women the same, or was she reading into my half-blindfolded expression and the heaving of my chest?

As I writhed under her, my arms and legs jerked uncontrollably, and the back of my head scraped against the pillow. I was afraid my wild movements would force the blindfold off, and when my head thrashed particularly hard, I closed my eyes. If it came off, she'd see it was an accident, that I hadn't been trying to look.

But despite how occupied she was with my breasts, she noticed as soon as the satin slid half an inch. After she readjusted it, the weight shifted on the bed beside me, and I guessed she'd sat down.

Apparently she was done torturing my nipples. The next assault was softer and silkier. It brushed over my thighs, then up to my belly before going all the way up to my chest and dusting over my well-abused nipples.

I had no idea what she was doing until I caught a whiff of a familiar spicy scent. Was that her hair? Was she dragging her long, gray-streaked mane all over my body? I'd never thought such a thing could be erotic, and yet the idea made me tingle even more than before.

"Please, Mistress..." I sounded needier, more sensual, than I'd ever heard myself before.

"Please what, Cherry?" Her hair swept along my mound, tickling it in erotic torment.

"Please, I need... you..."

"Where, my dear? And how?"

I quivered, painfully aware of how tightly my nipples had pebbled and how my unbelievable wetness was trickling onto my inner thigh. The cuffs, the blindfold, the torment – all of it was spiraling into a perfect storm of arousal. The pent-up tension in my core burned for release.

"I want you to go down on me," I managed. "Make me... make me come."

She was silent, and my anticipation built even higher. If she were to keep me waiting, I didn't how much more I could take. I was already at the end of my rope. A single brush of her tongue would shatter me.

I was starting to realize something about sleeping with Margo – it was becoming clear even from these first couple of times. The way she teased me brought its own version of pleasure, one tied up with torment and torture.

But that one moment, that one second, when she gave in? I lived for that. Every bit of frustration became worth it when she finally set her hands or mouth on me.

And that moment had finally come. Her hands grasped my hips, and her weight moved between my legs. I blinked up at the darkness under the blindfold as something heavenly brushed against my aching bud. My jaw fell open, and I let out a sound that was half-cry, half-moan.

The tension in my core built still higher. My limbs attempted to thrash, but the cuffs kept them maddeningly in place. Unused to being restrained like this, I opened my eyes to see what was happening – but the blindfold blocked every bit of light. And all the while, Margo continued swirling her tongue on my clit and around my entrance.

Oh God, she was still torturing me even as she gave me what I wanted. This was the most exquisite frustration I'd ever experienced. My hips arched up to meet her mouth – not too far, they weren't able to – and my legs shook in their restraints.

The tension built higher as Margo's tongue licked and swirled. The cries I was making were wild and desperate, and nothing I could do would hold them back. I was getting close, so close, but would I be able to push myself over the edge like this? Would I be able to come when I was unable to see or move?

She did something with her lips or mouth, something that made my toes curl and my core sing.

And I found the answer was yes. And yes, and yes again.

The orgasms ripped me apart… and when the cuffs were off and the blindfold removed, Margo was there to put me back together.

FOURTEEN

I stood in the barn, hugging my arms around myself. It was warm out, even now that all the work was done for the day and the sun was down. The chill was inside me. Today was the day Harmony would be slaughtered.

I bent down beside her, soaking in the sight of her narrow head and the two horns that pointed backward from her face. With her big brown eyes, she had to be the most innocent being I'd ever encountered. She was practically an angel.

"And you'll be one for real soon," I told her, my throat closing up and tears welling behind my eyes. "You'll be bringing sunshine and happiness to all the other animals up in heaven."

I caressed her soft fur. She was so beautiful – I couldn't understand how Margo could see her and think of what she could make out of her different parts, rather than seeing her for the whole and unique creature she was.

I'd been trying to remind myself that she was just an animal – but the "just" made less and less sense to me. I cared about this goat, so why would she be "just" anything? The more I thought about it, the more I believed I should give more respect to all animals rather than giving less to her.

"I wish I could get you out of this," I whispered. "That I could scoop you up and take you away from here, take you home with me… You might hate living in my apartment back home, but at least you'd be alive."

The worst part might be that she had no idea what was going on - no idea of the fate that was coming to her. She'd lived up to now in ignorant bliss. Now she had to be noticing my distress. When Margo came with the shotgun, she'd be terrified. I hoped the end would be painless for her. I hoped…

I couldn't think about this anymore. I wrapped my arms around her, feeling her fur against my skin, feeling her heartbeat and the breath running through her. For this moment, this single moment, she was mine. No one else could ruin this for me.

The sound of footsteps at the door made me look up. I kept hugging Harmony tight as Margo walked in. Unable to look at her shotgun, I squeezed my eyes shut and turned my head away. As sweet as she'd been to me, as many mind-blowing orgasms as she'd brought me to, right now I hated her with a passion. I wished she'd disappear.

"Oh, for fuck's sake." Her voice was exasperated. "Are you still on this?"

"I'm sorry." I couldn't explain my own reaction. "I'll get out of your way. I just wanted to say goodbye."

Letting out a long sigh, she came to my side. When I dared to look at her, her beautiful features were composed in a resigned expression. "I swear to God, I don't know why you're having such a hard time with this. I've had volunteers at slaughter time before, and they might not love the idea, but they do get used to it."

"I don't know why, either." Maybe it was because I'd come so close to death myself. "I swear I'll be okay with it, though. I don't like it, but I understand."

"You're still hugging her!"

I grimaced, not wanting to let go of the goat's softly breathing frame. I didn't want to even think about her going motionless, blood leaking out of a bullet hole in her head. But that was the way of life. I could make myself let go if I really tried. I could –

"Oh, for fuck's sake!" She sounded twice as exasperated as before. "I can't deal with this. If I slaughter her, are you going to mope around for the rest of your time here?"

A spark of hope lit in my heart. "Um… maybe."

"Get up." When I didn't move, she spoke louder. "Fuck it, Cherry, get up! I'm not going to hurt her." She stuck the shotgun under her arm.

"Really?"

"I must be fucking crazy, but yes." She was swearing more than I'd ever heard from her before, and the look on her face equally showed her frustration. The mean Margo from my first few weeks here was back, and yet completely different. "I'll wait until you leave. I don't give a fuck anymore."

"You'd do that for me?" My heart had been so heavy, and now all of a sudden, it was lightening. "Thank you… Mistress. Thank you so much."

"This isn't because I think killing a goat is bad or wrong," she said harshly. "I'm still going to slaughter her the minute you leave this farm. This is only a temporary reprieve because I don't want to see you being like… this… for the next month."

"Yes, that's fine. I understand." She did care about me!

"You're doing everything for her. Every single task. Feeding her, trimming her hooves, letting her in and out of the barn. I don't want to see her. I don't want to think about her."

"Of course, Mistress."

I let go of Harmony, giving her a good scratch behind the horns before I stood up. My whole body felt light, actually, as if a burden had been taken off me. And maybe Margo would change her mind again the next time she planned to slaughter Harmony.

"Come on, you." She put a hand on the small of my back as we walked out of the barn. "These damn city girls will be the death of me."

I was fine with her muttering. Harmony was safe, and that was all that mattered. "Are you going to cancel your party?" I asked.

"No… I'll buy a hank of beef and cook that instead." She shot me a glare. "Unless you'd prefer that we just serve vegetables."

"I'm fine with beef." Although I didn't intend to eat it.

"Good."

The rest of the night was taken up with preparations, and Margo drove to the grocery store in a nearby small town the next morning. She stood over the stove, braising the beef shank, while I quietly worked on some vegetarian side dishes.

"I see what you're doing," she said warningly. "Don't think I don't notice."

"I'm not doing anything. I'm just making some food."

By the time her guests started arriving, I'd made a green salad, a pasta salad, broccoli slaw, and brussels sprouts. I'd have plenty to eat without having to touch the meat.

We brought the food out to the fire pit. The night was dark aside from the fire and the moonlight. I tried to keep a smile on my face as Margo introduced me to one neighbor after another. I remembered Ed and Lewis, the wine makers she'd mentioned, and Sandra of the persimmon chutney. Other than them, I couldn't keep track of who was who as ten or twelve people filled up the log benches around the campfire.

"What's this?" Ed asked, examining the stockpot with the beef. "I thought we were having goat."

"Change of plans." Margo left it at that.

All of us sat around the fire, and the heat was welcome now that the night was progressing. I accepted a glass of wine that Lewis gave me, then served myself a plate from the table we'd set up. People were chatting animatedly, and Margo appeared to be having a great time.

Despite the lack of goat meat, everyone seemed happy to have an excuse to get together. A few of the guests complimented the dishes I'd made or asked how I was liking life on the farm. The community was as Margo had described it, friendly and welcoming.

I was the youngest one there, as I'd expected. Not by much, though. A few people were in their mid-to-late twenties. A younger couple told me they'd moved out here and started growing their own food to take a stand against climate change. They said it'd been quite a learning curve, but now they were self-sufficient and created close to zero greenhouse gas emissions, as well as zero waste.

I listened in awe. They led the type of life I would've aspired to if I'd ever been ambitious enough to even dream it up. I'd never known anything about going off-the-grid before I came out here. I always thought "reduce, reuse, recycle" was about as environmentally friendly as one could get.

I was particularly fascinated by Margo's sister. Like Margo, Sandra had a hippie vibe, although she was more feminine. She wore a flowing skirt with huge hoop earrings and blue eye shadow that glittered even by the firelight. Maybe this was what Margo would've looked like if she was straight.

When I'd been away from Margo for a few minutes, she glanced over at me. Seeing me alone, she sat at my side. I shivered slightly, so she put an arm around me and pulled me in. I wondered if she wouldn't mind the others knowing what was going on between us. We were only having a casual fling, I assumed she'd want to keep it private - but then she was so open about her sex life and her preferences. I decided to go along with whatever she did.

"Having a good time, sweet Cherry?" she asked.

"I am." I loved the feel of her arm around my shoulders. "You're not mad at me?"

"I was never mad at you. Mad at myself for putting both of us in this situation, maybe."

"Okay." A genuine smile came over my face, and I filled with relief - and a bit of desire, too. "The persimmon chutney was amazing, just like you said. The wine, too."

"Of course they were. I have excellent taste. I chose you, didn't I?"

I leaned into her embrace, content to soak up her approval. Nothing had changed from those first weeks - I still wanted nothing more than to please her. I hadn't realized until now how stressful butting heads over the Harmony issue had been. But here we were - we'd come through it, possibly stronger.

"What's this I see?" Sandra sat next to Margo and glanced from her to me. "Are you seducing your volunteers now?"

I'd started off liking Sandra, but now I wasn't sure how to take her comment.

"It's not like that," Margo said, squeezing my shoulders.

"Oh, no?" Sandra asked. "What is it like?"

"Cherry's trying new things right now," Margo said.

Sandra cackled. "And you're one of them?"

Margo cleared her throat, looking… embarrassed? I wouldn't have thought that was even possible. It seemed like she cared quite a bit about what her farming community thought.

Was that what she really thought of me, though? Of us? Sure, I'd come here to try something new - I could admit that plan wasn't the most well-thought-out. With her, though… I'd been curious about women and BDSM, yes, but it was so much more than that. I wasn't sure if it'd started that way or if it had turned into more somewhere along the line.

But she sounded fine with me "trying new things." She didn't want anything more than that.

"I'm surprised you finally fell victim to the temptation," Sandra said.

I frowned at that, not sure who or what she was referring to.

"We'll talk about this later," Margo said.

Apparently, her commanding tone worked on other people besides me. Sandra let out a sigh and rolled her eyes, but she changed the subject. "Anyway, how's the harvest looking this year?"

"Not bad," Margo said. "It helps having someone else around."

"Ah, so you actually get around to working between bouts of – "

"That's enough." Margo's embarrassed look was back, and she stood up. "I'm going to grab some more food. Cherry, go check if anyone wants more wine."

"Yes, Mis – " I caught myself in horror. "Margo."

I knew she was trying to cut the conversation short. Still, I wasn't going to risk not doing what she said. I went around asking if anyone needed more to drink, and when a few did, I fetched it for them. Everyone was so nice, I didn't even mind doing it.

I was dying to know what Sandra had meant by her comment, though. I wasn't going to disrespect Margo by asking Sandra, so I waited until the visitors had trickled home for the night. Although Margo was visibly tired, I didn't want to delay a second longer to bring it up.

"Why did your sister say that?" I asked, a step behind her as we both carried dirty dishes into the house. "About falling victim to temptation?"

"I knew you were going to ask about that." She shifted the dishes onto her hip so she could open the door. Once we were inside, she set them down on the kitchen counter with a clatter. "You've been worrying about that all night, haven't you?"

I couldn't lie to her. "Not all night, Mistress."

She chuckled, opening her arms to me. I went in for a comforting hug. "It's nothing bad, my dear. She knows that when you live in close proximity with someone for an extended period of time, things can happen. It's not uncommon for farmers to get involved with their volunteers during their stays."

"That's all?"

She shook her head. She kept holding me, silently telling me the dishes could wait until after this conversation. "She's also aware that a few of my volunteers have made attempts to become intimate with me in the past, and that I've always turned down their advances."

My throat tightened. I didn't like the thought of anyone else trying to "get intimate with" Margo – my Margo. "Why was that? Were they guys?"

"Some, yes, but they understood why I rejected them when I told them I was gay. Those that didn't, I asked to leave."

She was so casual about her past. These must've been rough experiences to go through, but from her tone, she could've been talking about the weather. Would she talk about me like that one day? What would she say?

I focused on my original question. "What about the girls? Why didn't you want to be 'intimate' with them?" I scratched my head. "They weren't kinky enough?"

"No." She gave a genuine laugh. "That's not all I require, you know. If I was compatible with every kinky female submissive, I'd have a world of options."

"What else is there?"

"You don't think there's more to our compatibility than that, Cherry? More of a reason that this has been working?"

"I… I don't know." I hadn't been sure that it had been working, from her perspective. She did seem fond of me, but I assumed she'd act like that toward anyone she was sleeping with.

"Any relationship, casual or not, should begin with a solid friendship," she said. "Two people have to get along, or they won't get far. They should know each other's moods, have enough things to talk about, be able to make each other laugh..."

"Oh, okay. That does sound like us." I pressed my head to her shoulder, keenly aware of her breasts moving as she breathed. I could have said all of that about Tyler when things were good between us, but it had fallen apart along the way. "So why did you change your mind when it came to me?"

"I suppose it's like Sandra said. I was tempted." She drew her thumb along my jaw. "I knew it might make things messy if it went wrong, especially with your lack of experience, but I couldn't resist. Why do you think I always call you my sweet Cherry? You were like the ripe, delicious fruit that you're named after, and you made my mouth water."

I felt warm inside. "I did?"

"Of course. The way you look at me when you ask about something you don't know about, the way you look up to me for my opinions... It gives me a huge rush."

Now my face was hot, too. "I thought you found it annoying."

"At first, maybe. Not anymore. And I think I made the right decision about this." She pressed a kiss to my forehead. "Don't you?"

"Yes, Mistress." I paused, wondering if this was a good time to bring up the other thing that was on my mind. She seemed more willing to talk openly than usual – maybe from having her friends over, maybe from the wine. "When will I get to do the same things to you that you do to me?" My face had to be bright red by the time the words were out.

She tensed up slightly, seeming surprised. "Sexually speaking? I hadn't thought about it."

"You told me you might want me to… to use the…"

"The strap-on, Cherry. You can say it." She laughed, her body relaxing as she squeezed me again. "Yes, that's true. I would enjoy that – eventually. Even though I'd still be the dominant partner, being on the receiving end can make me feel rather vulnerable. A certain level of trust needs to be established first."

I wished she trusted me already. "But I receive from you."

"And you're comfortable with that, aren't you?"

"More than comfortable." My insides tingled at the thought. "I guess you're right. We're doing what we're both good with." I hesitated, wondering if I'd come on too strong by saying what I really thought. Fuck it. "I do wish I could see you naked, though."

Her chuckle this time was low and dark. "All in good time, my sweet Cherry."

FIFTEEN

The summer was progressing at a rapid pace. I'd been on Margo's farm for two months now, and I could barely remember what the "real world" was like. I was more tanned than I'd ever been in my life – although the tan lines on my thighs and upper arms told a different story.

Harmony was happily living as a free goat, enjoying the pasture every day without being milked. To me, it seemed like a fitting reward for a life of service – even if Margo thought she'd be better off on the dinner table.

Taking care of Harmony had turned out to be more of a joy than a chore. In fact, I liked the responsibility of being her sole caregiver. The way she turned toward me when I came into the barn, the way she looked up at me with those big eyes… I could've been imagining it, but she seemed to understand there was a new connection between us. I certainly felt one.

When I thought about leaving this place, I got sad. Not just because of Harmony. In fact, it wasn't just because of Margo. I didn't want to leave this life. The fresh, homegrown food, the sun on my skin, the physical work, the early nights and early mornings… I'd gotten used to all of it. The lifestyle I'd adopted felt healthier than any I'd led before, and I felt a bit sick at the thought of returning to fast food and frequent drinking.

I looked at my watch as I squatted in the field, pulling out the weeds that threatened to choke the carrot plants. Eleven-thirty AM. If I were back in Omaha, I'd be in the end-of-morning meeting, getting praised for selling enough cars this week - or scolded because I hadn't sold enough. I'd be suppressing yawns as I drank my third cup of coffee of the day, fighting the heartburn the caffeine would bring on. I'd be peckish, too, dreaming of the McGrease Bomb I'd pick up for lunch.

With a life like that, it was no wonder I'd gotten sick.

"All good out here?" Margo called, a hand shielding her face from the sun as she approached me. "It's time to come in for lunch."

"Sounds good." One thing was the same as it had been before - I was starving. "I was thinking about making spicy enchiladas with the spinach we picked yesterday."

"All right. I'll fry some chicken for myself." She extended a hand to help me stand up. "I suppose I'm going to have to provide vegan meals for you for the next month."

"Um… maybe." I braced myself for the electric shock that always went through me when we touched. "I mean, probably. If that's okay with you."

She rolled her eyes – but I was pretty sure she did it affectionately. "Yes, I think I can deal with that."

I grabbed the bag I'd been putting the weeds in and jogged to keep up with her as she headed toward the house. "I was meaning to ask you, actually."

She slowed slightly. "What?"

"You know, I'm enjoying my time here, and I don't have a solid plan for what I'm going to do when I get home. I'm sure my subletter would be willing to stay a little longer, if… if you were willing to let me stay a little longer."

"You want to extend your stay?" She wiped the back of her hand across her forehead. "This isn't some cockamamie plan to keep me from slaughtering Harmony, is it?"

"Not at all. I mean… maybe a little bit." I was still getting used to not telling white lies with her. "But I want to stay. For the farm, and… for you."

That was as close as I'd gotten to telling her how I really felt about our relationship, and I waited breathlessly for her response.

"I suppose that would be fine," she said neutrally. "I can use the extra hands, and no one else contacted me about helping out this summer. Maybe another month or so?"

"That would be amazing! Thank you, Mistress." I stopped walking to wrap her in a bear hug.

She was tense in my arms at first, and then she relaxed. "You really wanted to stay, huh? You were pretty nervous about asking me."

"Yes."

She shook her head, linking her arm through mine as she started to walk again. "You shouldn't have been. If we can't be open and honest with each other, then what we're doing together could be downright dangerous."

"Okay, Mistress. I understand."

I practically skipped along the cobblestone path. I got to stay! Another month meant I had eight more full weeks here. Eight weeks to revel in the sun, and work hard, and play with Harmony… and explore every possible avenue of sensuality with Margo.

Eight weeks might not be anywhere near enough.

"This might be good, actually," she said as she opened the door for me. "You'll get to help out at the farmers market in August - that'll be interesting for you. And you'll get to harvest everything we've been planting and tending. I always think it's a shame when volunteers come for only part of the season. They put in all the work, and then they don't get the rewards."

The word "reward" sent an electric shock through my body. The other night, she'd tied me up and fed me strawberries as a reward for working hard all day. Between the taste of the fruit and her tasting me, it had been one of the most sensual experiences I could remember. This woman kept outdoing herself.

"That sounds great," I said. "Not to mention the other benefits."

"Like keeping Harmony away from certain death?"

"Yes, exactly," I teased. "That and nothing else."

"You're quite the little schemer."

"I may have to stay longer to make sure she stays alive," I said. "I may just end up staying forever."

Margo laughed and said nothing - which hurt a little. I hadn't expected her to say "Yes, Cherry, please do - move in with me and be my sub forever," but something would've been nice.

It was okay, though. She didn't feel the same as I did. That was clear, so I had to make myself accept it.

She could be fond of me, and she could give me numerous earth-shattering orgasms, and it could still all be casual to her. I was just another submissive in a long line of them, and that was fine.

When I left, I'd be a fun story for her to tell - the time she'd finally given in and hooked up with one of her volunteers. But guess what? She'd be the same to me.

Obviously I wasn't going to stay on a farm

forever. And I wasn't always going to be into kinky sex with women, either. I was still mostly straight and mostly vanilla. This was just a fun little diversion.

I had to keep telling myself that.

Later that night, I video called my sister to let her know I'd be staying here longer. Julie was stunned by the news.

"Why in the world would you want to stay longer?" she asked, her eyes widening on my phone screen. "Aren't you sick to death of dirt and stuff?"

I lay back on my bed, pulling the blanket over my legs. I wasn't completely sure if Margo was downstairs or outside, so I'd have to watch what I said. "The dirt isn't an issue. It does come off, you know."

"I've been told." Julie rolled her eyes. "I mean the whole thing, though. The plants, the animals, the work... Don't you miss bacon and cheeseburgers?"

"That's another thing. I'm vegan now." Her look of shock had me rolling with laughter. I gave her a quick explanation of the Harmony situation. "And no, I don't want any fancy vegetarian fake meat, either. I like the food here. It feels healthy."

"Since when do you care about being healthy?"

"Since I got here, I guess." I sat up again and shrugged. "I'm having fun and I'm learning things. The world can go on without me."

"Is this about your torrid lesbian love affair?"

I knew she was going to link it to that eventually. "I mean… maybe?"

"Are you serious?" she asked, gaping at me. "Wait, are the two of you serious? Are you a couple now?"

"No!" I hoped my face didn't betray how I really felt. "We're having some fun. A lot of fun. It's not a big deal. It'll end when I leave."

"You're blushing."

I pressed my fingers to my cheek. It did feel hot. "No, I'm not."

"So why are you staying longer?"

"Because I'm enjoying things! Jeez." I shook my head.

"Lesbian things?"

I huffed. "I swear to God, Julie, I'll hang up the damn phone."

"All right, all right." Although her tone was apologetic, she still smirked. "I'm trying to find out more about my little sister's life. Screw me, right?"

"Yeah, screw you." I snorted.

"Have you told Mom about your change of plans yet?" she asked, getting serious.

"Not yet." I leaned back against the wall,

spreading my legs across the bed. "You think she'll freak?"

"Probably. She's so worried about you already, and that's without even knowing you've been seduced by a dominatrix."

"Oh my God, I thought you were going to leave that topic alone." Despite my indignation, I was thrown off. I knew Mom wished I'd stayed home, where I could be close to medical attention if I needed it. Still, every time I talked to her, she seemed okay with me being here. "She won't be that upset, will she? She can deal."

"I don't know, Cherry. She's barely dealing as it is."

"Are you serious?" My stomach was tight. "I spoke to her the other day. She was joking around about me coming home with a pet goat. She knows I'm a grown adult and that I can take care of myself."

"Yeah, sure, and she also knows what you went through last year." Julie gazed at me seriously. "You may be an adult, but you're also her little girl. Always will be."

"Okay." She'd given me a lot to think about. "I'll give her another call soon and let her know I'll be back late. I'll make sure she knows everything is okay."

"All right. Don't be surprised if she wants to visit you out there and see for herself."

seductive purr.

I ran my fingers over my still-sore wrists, shivering. "That was amazing."

"Oh, yes? Did you like the vibrator better than my tongue? Be honest."

"Honestly, Mistress, I didn't." Although I'd gotten off, and majorly, I definitely preferred her herself over the silicone. Feeling her fingers and lips and tongue on me was simpler, more intimate, more satisfying. "But it was nice to change things up."

I ran my hands over her body. Over the past few weeks, I'd managed to get her out of her flannel shirts and down to the tight undershirts she wore underneath. She wouldn't take anything more off, not yet. Still, I got to touch much more skin than before, and I loved exploring the wiry muscles of her arms. All the farm work had made them well defined, even if her belly happened to be soft.

"How about changing things up in other ways?" I asked. "How are you feeling about that these days?"

"Are you talking about making me come?"

The edge in her voice ensured I'd give her a polite reply. "Yes, Mistress."

"Then say that." She squeezed my shoulder. "That might happen soon, actually."

"Oh-h-h," I said wonderingly. The throb she'd

just extinguished in my core started up again. I couldn't wait. "Soon like tonight?"

"Not quite." She laughed. "You're certainly eager."

"I just don't get why you wouldn't want it," I said. "Aren't you... horny?"

She brought her hand down to my hip. "Yes. I just have problems letting go. Not overthinking things."

"You?" I raised my eyebrows. She had to be one of the most confident people I'd ever met.

"Yes, me." She massaged my hip affectionately. "I told you, I need to trust a woman before I can allow her into my pants. I need to be sure I know her well enough. That she's the kind of person I want to be intimate with. Sex involves an intense exchange of energies, receiving more so than giving. If that person has the wrong energy, it can be dangerous."

"How?"

"Not physically dangerous," she clarified. "Emotionally."

"That makes sense." I did feel like I picked up some of her energy when we were "intimate." I'd picked up some of her beliefs and her patterns of speech just by being around her. "How long has it been since you've done that, then?"

"If I was counting, I'd say it's been five years

since I've been with anyone in any kind of way." She sounded oddly self-conscious. "And I am in fact counting."

"Five years? With all these people hitting on you? And you never decided to just do it for fun?" I propped myself up on an elbow so I could stare at her.

She looked mildly confused by my shock. "No, I wouldn't do that. I require more of a connection than that."

And yet here she was, sleeping with me. Even if it was one-sided for the moment, that still made me pretty damn special. A warmth soaked through me, heating up my chest. She'd told me she was fond of me before, but having hard evidence of that made it more real.

It's still only casual, the niggling voice at the back of my head reminded me. Don't get too happy about it.

I told the voice to shut up. "Well, whenever you think we have that connection, I'm right here," I said out loud. "For the next two months, anyway, so hurry up."

Her chuckle was low and somehow erotic. "You're that keen, are you?"

"Kind of." I let my gaze sweep down her body. "I'd like to try, seeing as how you've been so generous up to now. I'm sure I'll be terrible at first. That's another reason to get started – so I might be able to get halfway decent by the time I leave."

"Hmm." She arched her back, and the tank top she was wearing stretched over her breasts so that I could see the exact size, shape, and color of her nipples. "Maybe it's not such a bad idea."

"To let me try right now?" I flipped onto my knees, ready to tear her clothes off the instant she said the word "go."

"No. My God, you're like a dog trying to get a bone." She petted my hair, letting me know she was only teasing. "Tomorrow, perhaps."

My throat was dry. "That sounds good."

She climbed out of bed and headed to her bookshelf while I enjoyed watching her ass sway in the dim light. "That gives you a day to study up." She handed me a book.

The Whole Lesbian Sex Book.

I spent the next day poring over the book between bouts of work. Truth be told, I barely worked, darting off the field and back to the book whenever I got half a chance. The opportunity that had been given to me was a major one. I wanted to blow Margo's mind - but what if I fucked up and she never gave me another chance?

I learned a lot - from tongue tricks and finger maneuvers to the ins and outs of gender and gender presentation. I skimmed through the anal section, then jumped straight to the one on BDSM. But reading about it was a long way from reality. What if I didn't grasp the concepts? What if I failed at putting them into practice?

"Don't look so serious," Margo said, catching me sitting tensely with the book on the living room couch before dinner. Lunch had been late because I'd been reading, and dinner would've been too if I'd been cooking. "You should see the massive frown on your face right now."

"Is it cute, at least?" I tried to smile.

"I don't think you could not be cute – but I've seen better expressions on you."

"Fine." Dropping the book, I stood up. "Why don't we eat and I'll try to get this off my mind?"

"Really? You want to eat?" She quirked an eyebrow at me, grinning as she gestured at the book. "I thought you were chomping at the bit. We're finished our work for the day, so…"

My heartbeat sped up. "Are you offering?" I eyed her up and down, imagining what it'd feel like to finally slide her out of her clothes. I could practically feel her soft skin under my fingertips.

"Yes." She was as upfront as usual. "Are you up for it?"

"Um…" All my anxieties came flooding back to me. I'd been so eager to do this last night, but that was before I'd spent a whole day agonizing over it. "Maybe."

"There's no rush." She headed for the door.

"Wait!" I ran after her, my decision solidifying. I grabbed her shoulders before she could get out of the room. "I'll do it."

She spun me around, her lips flattening as she pushed me against the wall. "You speak like it's a chore, Cherry."

My breath came in gasps. She'd never manhandled me like that before - and I'd fucking loved it. Even now, she kept me pinned to the wall, one arm across my chest. "I'm sorry, Mistress."

"You better be." Her voice was dark and serious. "Even when I'll be on the receiving end, you'd do well to remember who's in control."

"I know, Mistress."

She backed off slightly, enough for me to embrace her. My heart was still pounding as I melted into the kiss. Her lips were soft yet demanding, and I did my best to accede to their demands. I stroked her hair, letting it out of its ponytail, then brought my hands to her hips as I kissed my way down her neck.

When I'd gotten a moan out of her, I unbuttoned her shirt, taking my time to spread the fabric apart and ran my fingers over her skin after each button. She was panting now, her lips slightly parted, the hair around her face growing damp with sweat. I could already see why she loved giving so much. If her reactions increased proportionally as we kept going, this would be extremely satisfying.

At last, I had her shirt open, and I slipped it off her shoulders. She had a more delicate bra than usual underneath, and the black material set off her tanned skin. I ran my hands over the cups, trying to find her nipples underneath.

She reached behind herself to unhook her bra, and her breasts came spilling out. I stared in astonishment. I'd imagined them so many times, and there they were in the flesh. And they looked a thousand times more delectable than I'd ever imagined. They sat low on her chest, perkier than I would've expected, propped up by the strong layer of pectoral muscle beneath.

I cupped one and ran my thumb over her pink, perfect nipple. She bit her lip, her eyes fluttering shut for half a second. Then –

"Get your shirt off," she said hoarsely.

"Why would I do that?"

"Because I'm telling you to, Cherry." Her tone brooked no disagreement.

My heart in my throat, I pulled my top over my head. When Margo nodded at my bra, I took that off, too.

"Good girl." She took my breasts into her hands, stroking them and then giving them a little lick. "Now lie down on the couch."

"What?"

"You had your fun." She squeezed my breasts, just hard enough for it to border on painful.

"Now it's my turn."

Although I still wasn't sure what she was planning, I went over to the couch. As I lay sideways, I watched her strip off her jeans. Because she'd just showered, she had no underwear on. My mouth watered as I spotted her bare mound.

She stepped toward me and climbed onto the couch, straddling my face. This would've been the perfect position for both of us to please each other, and a thrill went through me at the thought - except my pants were still on. I was already soaking through my panties. This might be its own form of torture.

"You read your book, my dear," Margo said, sounding breathier than I'd ever heard her. "You know what to do. Don't you?"

"Mm-hmm."

Gripping her hips, I stared up at her pussy - an intricate network of folds, a puzzle I had to decode. A bead of wetness dripped down her inner thigh, and I chose to lick that off first. She shuddered.

Maybe this wouldn't be so hard after all. I savored her flavor, musty and tangy, and gave her another lick in the same place. When I was rewarded with another shudder, I kissed her other inner thigh. She shook on top of me.

God, she was sensitive. And no wonder, if it'd really been five years. I smiled to myself. I knew

I could do this. I arched my head upward and licked all the way along one labia, then the other. I could hear her breathing getting ragged as I sucked each one into my mouth.

"Fuck... Cherry..."

She looked down at me, and I smiled back up at her. From down here, I could see her face through the points of her breasts. The effect was hot, and I fought the urge to touch myself. I was pretty sure that'd get me punished.

Gathering my courage, I tongued the junction where I thought her clit would be. There were more intricate folds, but I knew I was in the right area from the sound of her sighs. A bit of flesh slipped aside, and then a hard little nub was under the tip of my tongue. I'd found it.

Her whole body shivered above me. "Oh God, Cherry. That's the spot. Right there. Yes."

I kept licking, tentative at first - but as her hips rocked toward me and her hands gripped the couch arm on either side of my head, I realized I didn't need to hold back. I went at her with a passion, grabbing her hips, then her butt. My tongue darted in instinctive ways, as if I'd been meant to do this all along. When I thought about it, I tried to imitate the things she'd done to me that had really blown my mind. But it didn't seem to matter much. Whatever I did made her gyrate and shake more and more.

When I looked up at her again, her head was thrown back. As much as I could see of her face was transformed in an expression of pure bliss. I wasn't too far off myself. Even without anything touching my pussy, I was soaking wet and throbbing. I hoped it'd be my turn after this. Maybe that was selfish, but it was true.

"Oh fuck, Cherry, fuck. I'm getting close. I'm going to grind on you, is that okay?"

"Mmm." That was more than okay. That sounded like heaven.

Her hips moved back and forth in an urgent, sensual rhythm. As her moans got louder, her hips began to rise and fall. I held on, clinging tight, keeping my tongue pinned to her clit. She sounded frenzied now, cursing. A sheen of sweat rose under my hands.

Fuck, if she kept going this way, she'd knock both of us right over. Should I stop her? Use my safe word? What if we weren't going to fall and all I did was ruin her orgasm? I couldn't decide what to do. Her rapid gyrations brought my whole head and shoulders off the couch.

Did she realize what she was doing? She was moaning even louder, immersed in the throes of ecstasy. Her climax had to be imminent. I'd let her come and then I'd rearrange us safely before going in for round two. I could hold out another minute, even with my back sliding halfway off the couch.

At least, that was what I thought until her pelvis smashed against my head, knocking me backward.

My mouth slammed shut, my teeth digging painfully into my tongue. Immediately realizing something was wrong, she scrambled to get off me. But in her half-on, half-off the couch position, all she managed to do was fall.

And I fell straight after her. My torso twisted – and my head knocked against the floor, hitting the wood with a sickening crack.

Just like last time.

SEVENTEEN

The pain was excruciating. Although I was conscious, it took me a long moment to open my eyes. Margo crouched at my side, looking equal parts horrified and concerned. "Are you okay, Cherry?" she asked. "You had a bad fall."

I licked my lips slowly. "Need... the... ER."

"How do you know?" She held up a hand. "How many fingers am I holding up?"

I didn't bother to look. "Concussion. Had one last year." My voice was only a croak. "Took me... a year... to get better."

The next few minutes were a blur. Somehow she got both of us dressed and hauled me into her car. I struggled to keep my eyes open on the way to the hospital. I knew I had to - sleeping with a concussion could be dangerous, or worse. But I was groggy, so groggy. The lights of the other cars on the highway smeared into streaks, and everything else around me was fuzzy.

My head hurt. Rather than going away, the pain from the fall had transmuted into an ear-splitting headache.

Margo was silent even though I tried to talk to her - to apologize, to explain. I was vaguely aware that the sentences I was coming up with weren't making sense. I couldn't seem to put my words in the right order.

Finally the two-hour drive to Green Root was over. I stumbled out of the car, leaning on Margo. She brought me inside, and I was vaguely aware of the front desk nurses talking to her, asking what had happened to me.

They gave me a room right away, and another nurse came in to find out more about my condition.

"Seems to be a concussion," Margo said. "She fell and hit her head."

The nurse nodded and started to leave.

"She had one before, if that makes a difference. About a year ago, I – I think." Even to my foggy mind, she sounded less confident than I'd ever heard her.

"Do you know any other details about it?"

"No. She didn't tell me." Her frustration was clear now. "She didn't tell me anything."

The nurse turned to where I sat at the edge of the hospital bed. "Hi there, I'm Nurse Yee. Can you tell me what happened?"

"Fell." I wet my lips. I'd wanted to say I fell.

"How did that happen?"

I was silent for a long moment, thinking. "Sex."

To her credit, the nurse didn't blink an eye. "Okay. Can you tell me your name?"

This one took me even longer. Of course I knew my name, so why couldn't I think of it? God, my head hurt so badly.

I pictured a red fruit dangling from a slim, delicate stem. It was... it was a... "Cherry."

"Good," Nurse Yee said. "And do you know what day it is?"

"Um..." It took me a long moment to remember we'd finished work for the week, that we were supposed to be taking it easy for the weekend. "Friday."

"Do you know what date of the month?"

I hesitated. "I never know that. I live on a farm." My words didn't sound quite right. I was slurring.

Nurse Yee glanced at Margo, who nodded slightly. "All right," the nurse said. "You certainly seem to have a concussion, but it doesn't seem too severe. Can you tell me about the last time this happened?"

I nodded slowly. Surprisingly, the story was less blurry than everything else. Maybe because it'd constantly been on my mind for the past year.

The words didn't come out the exact way I hoped for them to. The gist was something like this.

Last summer, I was at a pool party with my ex-boyfriend and some friends. The day was sunny and warm, and we were a bunch of young adults drinking. A friend had just turned twenty-one and wanted to enjoy her first legal drink. She invited us over to her parents' house. There was no lifeguard, obviously. No one to tell us how dumb we were being.

I was four or five tequila shots in, and I was on top of the world. People were jumping into the pool, or pushing each other in. I spent most of the afternoon reclined on a lawn chair, tanning, but my friends kept calling me to get up, to jump in with them. God, I wish I'd stayed.

I started a few yards back from the pool. People had been saying the water was cold, so I wanted to submerge myself all at once. I was going to cannonball in. So I ran.

"Don't run by the pool." Any kid knows that.

Somehow, I forgot.

I made it about a step and half, and then I slipped and cracked my head on the floor.

I woke up in the hospital what felt like an eternity later. They told me only half an hour passed. I was seeing double, I couldn't think straight, I couldn't focus on anything. My head was throbbing, and I couldn't stand up without wanting to puke.

Within a couple of hours, I had the all-clear to go home. But I wasn't better. I still got confused about the simplest things. I wasn't supposed to do "mentally demanding" activities. Bright lights left me in unspeakable pain, and even the normal lights at my apartment were unbearable. Loud noises were just as bad. Just standing up made me dizzy. I had no idea when I'd be able to go back to work, much less return to a normal life.

At first I told myself I just had to wait it out. If I could tough it out for a week, I'd be okay. But after a week, not much was better. Not even after a month. The symptoms wouldn't go away. I couldn't focus my eyes on a book. Couldn't stand to squint at a computer. There wasn't much I could do. I spent a lot of time lying in bed or spacing out in front of the TV.

My friends came to visit… until they stopped. Maybe it was because I wasn't replying to their texts. Maybe because I was depressed and unresponsive when they saw me. I was a shitty friend - I'd admit that readily. I wouldn't have wanted to be around me, either.

The doctors started talking about "post-concussion syndrome." For most people, concussion symptoms were gone in a matter of weeks. For others, like me, they lasted far, far longer than they should, and there was no clear reason why.

Sometimes I tried to comfort myself by accepting the situation. Every time I went back to the doctors, they said they couldn't help. If this was my new normal, then I had to get used to it. If I ever did get better, though? I wasn't going to continue on the path I'd been on before.

Tyler had been a saint – acting more like a home aide than a boyfriend, and never complaining. Still, after that first month passed, I opted to move back in with my parents. Once I was with them, I could sink lower into my depression. Life didn't seem worth living when I could hardly do anything. When would my symptoms go away?

My mom couldn't stand to see me like this – a shell of my former self. She took charge of my health care. When the doctors told her they couldn't help, she wouldn't take "no" for an answer. She had them test me and retest me.

And finally, after months, we found an answer. I had a blood disorder. That was why my concussion had been so much worse than it should've been, why I hadn't recovered in the two to four weeks I should've recovered. The trauma of the injury had caused my brain to bleed, and all these months later, it was still bleeding.

Now that we knew what was wrong with me, there were new options to treat me. I stopped myself from getting my hopes up, and for good reason. Even with the new diagnosis, it still took months before I returned to anything resembling normal function. I took baby steps, going to the corner store by myself and then taking the bus.

As the light appeared at the end of the tunnel, a plan began to crystallize in the back of my mind. Once I got through all this, I wasn't going to be the same person anymore. I needed to care about more things than selling cars and having fun. I needed to become a better person, and to do something good for the sake of the planet.

By the time I came to my recitation, I was exhausted. My words had been slow and slurred, and certainly not as eloquent as they were in my mind. Still, I'd gotten them out.

Nurse Yee nodded, taking notes on her clipboard. Margo's gaze was on the floor.

Despite the pain I was in, I felt like a burden had been lifted off me. I'd spoken my truth, and I was finally free.

"That's all," I whispered. "Can I sleep?"

"You can rest, my dear. The doctor will be in to see you in a moment." Nurse Yee slid her pen into her pocket and left.

"My dear" was Margo's affectionate name for me. I glanced over at her, looking for a clue as to how she felt in her face.

I hoped and prayed she wouldn't pity me - wouldn't see me as some broken invalid.

But in fact, there was no expression on her face. None at all.

EIGHTEEN

I slept like the dead. It could've been hours or days later when I opened my eyes to see an all-too-familiar face at the foot of my bed.

"Mom?" I started to jump up to hug her, then stopped short from the blinding pain. I couldn't have gone far with the IV that was now in my arm, anyway. "What are you doing here? How did you get here?" My words were still slow. I sounded stupid.

Although Mom seemed happy I'd woken up, her face was drawn. "The lady you work with, Margo, called me. She said you gave her my number as an emergency contact. I took the first flight out, then rented a car at the airport."

"Oh, God." She'd gone to so much trouble, all because of my own stupidity. Hours and hours of travel, and she must've spent so much money, too. "I'll pay you back for the flight."

"As if I care about the money!" She sat heavily beside me and wrapped me in a hug. "I thought I'd seen you in a hospital for the last time."

"Surprise," I said weakly.

She shook her head. Her face was an older version of mine and Julie's - both of us had gotten her high cheekbones and dark eyebrows.

At the moment, she looked twenty years older than she was. It was like looking in a funhouse mirror at my seventy-year-old self.

"Seriously, Cherry, how did this happen?" she asked. "You know how terrible things went for you last time. Why would you ever, ever put yourself at risk of going through all of that again?"

I couldn't come up with a lie on the spot. "I don't remember how it happened. I'm sure I couldn't have seen it coming."

"Margo said you hit your head on a roof beam."

"Oh, yes. That."

I winced as a shot of pain pulsed through the back of my skull. In a concussion, the brain collided directly with the skull. I was pretty sure I could feel the exact spot where it'd happened.

So she'd met Margo – the thing I'd thought would never happen. And I hadn't been there to see it. What had they said to each other? What had they thought of each other? More importantly, where was Margo now?

Thinking too hard made my head hurt. Even if this concussion wasn't nearly as bad as the last one, this was still far from pleasant.

"How could you do that to yourself?" Mom asked. "Why wouldn't you be careful? I knew it was a bad idea to let you come all the way out here by yourself. I should've talked you out of it. You could've died out here. It took you two hours to get to medical care. If that blow to the head had been worse… My God, Cherry." She hugged me again.

The last few weeks before I left, we'd gotten back to something approximating our normal relationship - joking around, speaking openly, respecting each other as adults. Now, though, she was back in full-on helicopter-mom mode. She may have had a point, but I still rankled at how overbearing she was.

I wanted to ask if she wanted me to go around wearing a helmet twenty-four-seven. There was no way I could get the words out as snarkily as I wanted them - and besides, she'd come all the way here for me. I let her hug me, and when tears formed in my eyes, I didn't fight them.

"I'm sorry," I whispered.

I should've taken better care of myself. Letting Margo go crazy like that, in that position - it was damn near idiotic. Even if I hadn't had the pre-existing head injury, I would've gotten badly hurt.

"Okay, baby," Mom said, squeezing my hand. "Relax for a little while. I don't want to stress you out."

I licked my lips. "Where's Margo?" My voice was barely a whisper.

"She had to go back to the farm. She said something about a goat."

Oh God, Harmony. A wave of guilt coursed

through me, and I closed my eyes.

Mom must've taken it as pain. "Rest up. You'll feel better soon, very soon."

I let my head press down into the pillow. "When's Margo…" I didn't have the energy to finish the sentence.

Mom understood anyway. "She'll be back tomorrow, sweetie. Visiting hours are from ten to four. She didn't say exactly when she'll come."

I swallowed. "Okay."

I rested as best as I could. The IV was a constant distraction - although I would've been distracted anyway. Like last time, I couldn't concentrate too well.

In fact, everything had an odd déjà vu feeling to it. The hospital room, white and sterile. The nurses bustling in and out. My mom, napping in the chair to one side. Even though we were in a different state, so much was exactly the same. At least this time, the other bed was empty. I had the room to myself.

An orderly in blue scrubs came to the door with a meal tray. "Cherry Highton?"

"Yes." I tried to sit up again, then collapsed back down. Seeing the food had made me realize I was starving.

The orderly handed me the meal and left. I fumbled at the juice box, unable to get it open.

Mom took the tray for me and helped.

I took a long sip, feeling the liquid rush through my body. "This is good." It was still a struggle to speak.

"Which do you want first?" Mom asked. "The mashed potatoes or the meatloaf?"

I looked in horror at the tray. "I can't. Vegan."

"Since when?" She glared at me. "That woman was trying to tell the staff you'd want a vegan meal. I thought she was making it up. Of course you need meat." She opened the meatloaf and forked up a bite. "Come on now. It'll make you strong."

Visions of Harmony danced through my head. "No."

" Are you serious?"

I nodded.

"You can't just eat juice and corn."

This argument was exhausting me. I couldn't think straight enough to respond. I lay back, closing my eyes.

"Maybe I can still get you a vegan meal," she muttered.

When she came back a few minutes later, she'd managed to find me one. I ate slowly, struggling to feed myself while lying down. I might have been a mess, but I wasn't quite at the point of letting my mom spoon-feed me.

Eventually I had to rest my eyes for a minute - and when I woke up, Margo was there.

I stared at her, stunned. Maybe it was the brain injury, but she looked like some kind of angel. With sunlight streaming onto her from the window, her tanned skin shone and the gray streaks in her hair sparkled like silver. She was a thousand times more stunning than usual - and usually she was pretty damn stunning.

I shifted toward the edge of the bed, drawn toward her as if by a magnet. Would it be dangerous to kiss her in my condition? Usually her kisses made me feel like my head would explode, so maybe right now that could actually happen.

It took me too long to realize she wasn't wearing her usual warm expression. On the contrary, her face looked… cold.

"Hi, Cherry." Not her sweet Cherry. "Feeling any better?"

"Yes." I reached a hand toward her. She glanced at it and didn't take it in hers. My throat tight, I let my hand flop back to my side.

"That's good. You gave me quite a scare."

"Me, too." I kept my sentences short, hoping she wouldn't notice just how badly I'd fucked myself up.

"I heard you managed to get yourself a vegan meal."

"Yes." I wanted to thank her for advocating for me in the first place.

"I can't keep coming back to visit you. I'll bring your things next time. You can take them with you when you go home."

I tried to sit up again, and pain jolted through the back of my skull. I ignored it. "What?"

"You lied to me," she said simply. "I asked you about medical conditions. You told me you had none. If I had known, I would have been much more careful with you. There were so many things that could have hurt you. And something like this…" She gestured at me. "It could have gone so much worse."

"But… Margo…" I reached for her again, my heart breaking into pieces.

"You could have died, Cherry," she hissed. "Because of your own deceit. And who would've been to blame? Me."

"I – I'm sorry." My throat was choked, and tears were forming behind my eyes.

"I don't forgive you." Her expression was terrifying in its coldness. "Leaving aside the danger of it all, I thought I knew you. I was wrong. You didn't share the most transformative experience you had – the thing that dominated the past year of your life. I trusted you, and for what?"

My body tingled as I remembered what had happened when I'd finally gained her trust – but the tingles stopped when I thought about where that trust had gotten her.

I couldn't be eloquent right now. "I'm sorry," I whispered again. I couldn't tell her how sorry I was. I needed to have this discussion later, when I could both think straight and express myself. "We'll talk later?"

Slowly, she shook her head. "I don't think so." She stood up, deftly avoiding the hand that I again reached toward her. "Thank you for all your hard work on the farm, Cherry. I appreciate all the effort you put in."

Oh God, she was serious. Her tone, her face - everything was so chillingly cold.

"Please," I whispered.

But she was walking out of the door.

She was gone.

NINETEEN

I begged Mom to get a hotel room with me when they let me out of the hospital. Margo may have never wanted to see me again, but I still held onto my hope that she'd forgive me. And there was no way that'd happen if I was halfway across the country.

I didn't tell Mom why I wanted to stay in Idaho. I still hadn't told her about the relationship - or whatever I was supposed to call it. So her initial response was a firm "no." She'd already taken several days off work, and she wanted to get back home and return to normal life as quickly as possible.

Then I looked into flying with a concussion. The evidence didn't specifically say it would be harmful, but several websites did mention they could give you a bad migraine. With that argument, I managed to convince her to stay for one night.

I wasn't sure what my game plan was. I just knew I didn't want to be hundreds of miles away from Margo.

"After this, you'll come home with me, of course," Mom said with a sniff as we went into the hotel. "You had your fun going back to the land or whatever. That lasted long enough. It's time that you come home and get back to your actual career."

The room was airy and bright, which at the moment was giving me a headache. At least there were two beds, each covered with a thick duvet. The beds looked soft and comfortable. After months of the shitty bed at Margo's and then the hospital bed, I couldn't wait to collapse onto one.

"Mom, I'm done with car sales." I could talk a little more now, although it still made my head hurt worse.

"Then you'll find another job." She dropped her duffel bag on one of the beds. "Maybe give Tyler a call, too. I'm still in shock that you ended things with him."

"I'm glad I did." I hardly even thought about him anymore. I was sure he'd moved on, too.

"Well, what are you planning to do when you get home?"

I sat heavily on my bed. "I don't know." I hadn't planned anything. "I just want to rest."

"You have to think about these things, Cherry. You took some time off, but that was never going to last forever. There was always going to be a next step."

I was silent. She was wrong. All I'd wanted was to stay on Margo's farm and be with her. Keep loving her.

Mom went gentler. "You must be tired. Lie down, and we'll talk later."

"Okay."

I got under the covers, but I couldn't sleep. All I could think about was Margo. Even in my brain-damaged state, I understood why she'd broken things off with me. I'd lied to her from the start, even when she'd asked me direct, simple questions.

Would it have been so bad if she'd known about my condition? Yes, she would've pitied me – but given how blunt and straightforward she was, I didn't think she would've babied me. She would've been more careful with me for sure… and I might not be in this position right now.

I rolled from side to side on the bed, unable to settle myself down. The thing that nagged at me was that Margo didn't know about my feelings for her. She didn't return them, obviously… except what if she did?

Lying there, I went over every interaction with her I could remember. The conversations, the joking, the sex, the cuddling. I remembered her deciding not to kill Harmony for my sake.

Wasn't there a chance that she felt something for me? Even if I couldn't be sure, wasn't that chance enough to not give up?

Because if she felt something, then she might forgive me.

I had been special to her. She'd gone five years

without sex, and she'd chosen me to break her dry spell. She'd trusted me.

Connections that special were rare and valuable, and personally I'd do anything in the world to keep from breaking one. Wouldn't she do the same?

"Why are you so restless?" Mom asked, sounding irritated.

Giving up on sleeping, I pulled the cover down. "I have to tell you something."

I kept my explanation short, telling her only that I'd been dating Margo - and that I wanted to keep doing so.

She was shocked, naturally. She'd never had any idea I was interested in women, mainly because I hadn't been before Margo. And while I didn't tell her about the kinky aspect, she was also taken aback by the age difference.

"When were you going to tell me all of this?" she asked, seeming hurt. "What else has been going on behind my back?"

"Mom, I need you to focus on what's important." I needed her to chill the fuck out.

"Fine." She paused for a long moment. "Does Julie know about all of this?"

I cringed. "That's different!"

She glared at me until I shrank back and looked away. "So now she's mad at you," she finally said. "What do you expect me to do about it?"

I blinked against my splitting headache. Talking so much had made it ten times worse. "I need to go to her. Make her understand."

"But you already talked to her," she said. "Why would she have changed her mind?"

I shrugged. I didn't expect her to change her mind. I just wanted to make sure I wasn't giving up too soon, while I might still have a chance.

"It's a two-hour drive," Mom said, looking irritated. "It's not like you'll be able to drive yourself. You're asking me to drive four hours on the off chance that this woman will forgive you?"

I did my best to look as pathetic as possible - not a difficult task at the moment. "Please, Mom."

She heaved a sigh. "Why don't we call her?"

I bit my lip. That could be a viable middle ground. I would've preferred to see Margo in person, where she couldn't just hang up on me. But I doubted I could talk my mom into that.

"What would we say?" I asked.

"There's no 'we,' first of all. You're going to do the talking." She huffed at me. "You're a little past the point of begging your mommy to fix things for you. As for what you're going to say, you know her better than me. What do I know? I don't even understand what your plan is. If she takes you back, do you intend to just live on this farm forever?"

My throat closed up. "I don't know." I hadn't thought that far ahead. I just wanted to be there now, and to stay for as long as I could.

"Well, you'd better think of something fast." She dug my phone out of her purse and held it out to me. "You want to call her? Call her."

I stared at the phone, my heart pounding. "But what do I say?"

She unlocked the phone and skimmed through the contacts list. "You said her name is Margo?"

"Yes, but..."

She'd already pushed the dial button. She put the phone on speakerphone and shoved it at me.

Margo picked up after two rings. "Cherry?" Her voice was flat.

"Hi." I took a deep breath, really more like a gasp. "I'm sorry. I don't want to bug you. I just..."

Just wanted to tell you I love you? To apologize for being a piece of shit? To beg you to take me back?

"I just wanted to know if Harmony is all right."

There was a long pause, so long I thought she might've actually hung up. I checked the phone screen to see if the call was still going on.

"Yes," she said stiffly. "She's fine."

A whoosh of breath escaped me. Harmony was alive – Margo hadn't slaughtered her. That meant she wasn't totally hardened. She had some affection left... possibly for Harmony... possibly for me.

"That's great," I said. "Um... do you think I could come see you sometime? I'd like to talk to you."

"I don't know what there is to say that hasn't been said."

Fuck, she was killing me. "I'll come anyway, if I won't be imposing on you."

She let out a sigh. "Fine. Tomorrow. Come after work hours."

"Okay. Perfect. See you then." I couldn't stop smiling as I hung up.

Now I had just over a day to figure out how I was going to get there.

In the end, Mom got sick of my worrying and whining. She said she'd take another day off work and drive me out there. She was an insurance salesperson, so no one was going to suffer from her being gone a little longer – other than her pocketbook.

She didn't say it, but I felt like she was trying to show me support in her own way. She wouldn't have driven me two hours in each direction if she had any issues with my newfound sexuality.

Of course, part of me hoped I'd be making a one-way trip.

At three o'clock exactly, we loaded our stuff into

her car. The ache in my head had faded to a dull throb, and when I stayed still it sometimes even disappeared. I could even look at the mid-afternoon sun without wanting to die. This was definitely a thousand times easier than my last concussion.

We talked on and off during the drive. Mom seemed to want to fill the silence, even when doing so made my head hurt. Granted, she hadn't seen her youngest daughter in a couple of months - but damn, I really didn't need to hear about Uncle Jimmy's tooth extraction. She asked me about life on the farm, too - but mostly she just talked.

As we got closer to Margo's place, I started to become glad for the distraction. Her chatter kept me from thinking about how angry Margo was at me and how unlikely it was that I'd be able to get her to forgive me.

Even the conversation couldn't keep the drive going forever. Eventually, the countryside began to look familiar. We were getting closer and closer to Margo's place.

At last, Mom pulled the car to a halt at the edge of the property. "You do what you need to do," she said. "I'll wait for you here."

I nodded. Carefully, I stepped out of the car. My first stop was the barn. I needed to see Harmony - not to mention to pull myself together before I went up to Margo.

But Margo's shadowy form was the first thing I

saw when I entered. "Somehow I knew this would be your first stop," she said, standing up from Harmony's feeding trough.

I looked from her to Harmony and back again, struck by such a powerful feeling of love that I didn't know what to do with it. The goat knickered softly when she saw me, and I ran over to pet her. I would've run to Margo first if I thought she'd accept it as readily.

"I see where your priorities lie." She stood back, crossing her arms.

Was it my imagination, or did she sound a little softer than last time? Was she warming up to me the tiniest bit?

"Margo…" I swallowed hard. Now that I was finally here, her beauty dazzled me, and I couldn't remember any of the hundreds of things I'd wanted to say. "I'm sorry."

"You said that already." She stayed where she was, unmoving.

I took a couple of hesitant steps toward her. The main thing I'd wanted out of coming here was to tell her how I felt – so I gathered every shred of courage that I had and decided to do just that.

"I fucked up." I placed one hand on her arm, and she didn't move away. "I thought you'd see me differently if you knew. I thought I'd lose your respect, and I couldn't stand to do that. I wanted to please you more than anything – anything – else."

She watched my face closely, as if she suspected what was coming. "Why?"

"Because I love you, Margo." I swallowed again, dropping my gaze. "It isn't just sex anymore. I don't know if it ever was. It's definitely not just about the kink. I care about you more than I ever thought I'd care about anyone. You turned my life upside down and shook all the bad stuff out. You made me a whole new person, and I like who I am when I'm with you. I don't want to be that other girl."

She said nothing.

I rubbed her arm, hoping against hope that my words were getting through to her. "I couldn't stand the thought of never seeing you again. I still can't. Do you know what would happen if I went home and left you here? I wouldn't have a normal life to go back to. I'd never become the person I used to be. I'd just be a shell of myself - and spend the rest of my days thinking and dreaming about you."

Finally we met each other's eyes. "Cherry…"

I shook my head. "Don't say you don't feel it, too. I don't know if you love me, but you care. You do, or this goat wouldn't be standing here." I gestured at Harmony, who bleated on cue.

Margo's lips twitched, and I had a powerful urge to kiss them. I resisted, not wanting to push too far, too fast.

"You don't have to say everything I said back to

me," I told her softly. "I wanted that to be out in the open, in case… in case it changes anything."

She let out a sigh, and her hand moved to the back of her neck. "What do you want from me, Cherry?" she asked. "What's your ideal outcome here?"

My throat went dry. "I'd like to finish my stay here, if you'd have me. We can see how things go." My feelings for her would be out in the open, even if hers were still a mystery.

"And then what?" she asked, peering into my eyes. "What happens when your time is up?"

My voice got smaller. "We already agreed I'd stay longer. We could do that again."

"So, what?" she asked. "You stay until farming isn't fun anymore? Until you fall out of love with me?"

"No… I…"

She shook her head. "This is why I don't date city girls. I knew you'd want to go back." She moved to the side of the barn and tidied something on a shelf. Her words seemed like she was muttering to herself more than to me. "It'll never work, Cherry. This isn't your life. You're just playing pretend."

"I'm not!" The words came out more high-pitched than I expected. "I want to be with you. I want to live here. I love it here, and I feel like…" I took a deep breath. It was so hard to spill my guts like this when I had no idea how she felt herself. "Like this is what I've been searching for. Like I was running around my whole life, looking for the spot I could call my own, and here… I feel like finally found my home."

"This is my home." She was glaring at me now. "I built it from the ground up using my own two hands, and you? You came here and lied to me."

I grimaced. "That's fair. Let it out. If you're mad, that means you feel something."

"Go fuck yourself, Cherry." She stormed toward the door of the barn.

I rushed after her, pain lancing through my forehead. "Wait. Just tell me… do you love me? Do you feel anything?"

She stopped just ahead of the door. "I could've. Not anymore."

"Stop." I grabbed her arm before she could go any farther. "That means there's something there. We both know there is. Don't run away from me. Let me stay, and I'll do anything in the world to make it up to you."

Her eyes glittered at me. "Anything?"

I nodded vehemently. "Yes."

Her lips ticked up with the hint of a smile. "Yes, who?"

The skin along the curve of my spine prickled into goosebumps. My breath came in hot, shallow gasps.

"Yes, Mistress."

Twenty

It turned out that the first thing Margo wanted me to do was get better. Even before I came back, she'd been looking into what to do after a concussion - and more hope sparked in my heart when she told me that.

Given the issues with flying, she said it was better for me to stay right where I was. I wasn't forgiven, she reminded me, but we'd work all of that out once I was healed.

I went back to the car and told my mom what was going on. While she was reluctant to leave, she eventually accepted that this was what I was doing. I gave her a big hug and thanked her for coming here. She'd been a lifesaver over the past few days.

"Give Julie a hug for me when you get back," I told her. I didn't know when I was going to see my big sister again.

The next few days passed slowly, dreamily. At first, I lay in bed, not doing much. Margo would sit next to me when she wasn't working, reading to me from some of her fantasy books. As time passed, she said I could start pushing myself a tiny bit more. She gave me a pack of cards to play Solitaire and showed me some light yoga stretches I could practice.

Other times, I went for long, slow walks around the property. There was so much to explore, and I couldn't get enough of the natural beauty. Once Margo cleared me to go into the barn, I visited Harmony every day, too. The goat always seemed content to see me, and I loved the affectionate way she'd butt me with her horns.

Since the farm took so much of Margo's time, I had a lot of space to myself. There were long periods when I didn't do much but think. Making my brain work still hurt, so I didn't think about anything too strenuous. Mostly I just ruminated on how much I loved Margo and how well she was taking care of me.

I didn't know what she had in mind for when I was better, but I'd do whatever it took to prove myself to her.

After a few days, she said I could start helping with the farm work again. "Only the easy stuff," she told me. "You're not going to exert yourself."

"What if I want to exert myself?" I asked, lacing up my shoes. "There isn't that much easy stuff."

"Trust me, I'm going to keep you busy."

And she kept her word. She heaped task after task on me, half of them clearly pointless. She had me watering trees even after it rained, spreading mulch where it'd already been spread, pruning plants that were solely decorative…

This was clearly the equivalent of the busywork that teachers used to give me in elementary school. But I trusted she had her reasons, even if that was just to keep me outside in the fresh air and sunshine. I was still here, so I couldn't complain.

After almost a week had passed, she caught up with me in the barn. I'd been petting Harmony, and I let go of her spotless white fur as Margo approached.

"You must be doing better," she said. "You're already obsessed with that goat again."

"I don't think I ever stopped." I ran a finger along Harmony's horn. "But yeah, I'm much better. Almost back to normal."

She stepped closer to me, and my heartbeat picked up speed. "I was worried, you know. You gave me a real scare… especially when I heard the full story of your first concussion."

She hadn't talked this openly with me all week. "I should've told you," I said softly. "It wasn't right of me to keep that from you."

"That's a given." She paused, her eyes searching mine. "I wonder how it is that this concussion affected you so much less. Recovering in a week rather than a year, and usually repeated concussions are so much worse than single ones."

I'd thought about that, too. "I hit a different part of my head this time," I said, gently touching the spot where my skull had made contact with the ground. "And it had been a long time since the first concussion. And..."

"And?" She quirked her eyebrows up.

I bent next to Harmony again, looking down at her as I stroked her soft fur. "And I have more to live for now," I said. "When I read about post-concussion syndrome, it said it's affected by your state of mind. If you're depressed or if you have bad coping skills, your recovery will be worse."

"Were you depressed?"

"I didn't think so, but maybe I was." My throat was tight. "I didn't realize how miserable I was, how pointless my life was. My job, my relationship - everything was what society wanted from me, but it wasn't right. I wasn't happy."

"Your mother told me..." The seriousness of her voice made me look up to meet her eyes. "She said there were times when she was afraid she'd find you bleeding out in the bathtub or overdosed on pills. She said she's never seen anyone struggle so much with anything."

I'd never known Mom thought I would kill myself. "It was bad, but not that bad."

"She didn't know." Margo shrugged. "She said in your position, the thought would've crossed her mind, too. She was amazed at the strength within you."

She took another step closer, and the heat of her body made heat rise within mine. Fuck, I missed her so much. She hadn't touched me at all since the accident, and while my sex drive had gone away at first, it was coming back with a vengeance.

"Everything is better now," I whispered. "I found something to live for."

Her hand came down on my shoulder, and I shivered at the sudden contact. "This past week… you haven't been bored? You haven't wished you'd gone home?" She seemed uncertain - nervous, even.

Quickly, I shook my head. "Not for one second. I love being here. I love being with you." I paused for a moment. "I love you," I finished quietly.

She kept quiet for another moment, just looking at me. "I love you too, Cherry. I don't know how or why or when it happened. I thought I'd closed myself off from all of that long ago, but somehow you slipped under my defenses."

My heart jumped. "I have no idea how I managed to do that."

"And yet you still did." She shook her head slowly. "I should hate you for how you lied to me, but… I don't. Maybe I would've if all of this hadn't happened, but all I can think about is that you came back. A city girl, an urbanite. Even after being in town, seeing your mom, having the chance to go home… you came back."

"Because I want to be here," I said. "With you. Nothing else matters."

"It doesn't, does it?" Her full lips quivered. "Come here."

She pulled me in, staring into my eyes for a second before planting her mouth on mine. The world spun as if I'd hit my head again. She always did leave me dizzy and breathless – but in the most incredible possible way.

As I laced my arms around her neck and parted my lips to allow her tongue inside, I wondered once again how I'd ever been uncertain about being with a woman. I didn't know if I ever would've or could've been interested in other women, but being here, with her – it felt like coming home.

I groaned into her mouth as the kiss deepened and intensified. My core was pulsating now, my wetness dripping through my panties. I heard myself let out a whimper, and was almost embarrassed at my own neediness – until I realized Margo was breathing just as hard, just as raggedly.

"Shall we go to the bedroom, my sweet girl?" she asked, running a finger along the neckline of my top.

"Yes," I said. "Yes, please."

Lacing our fingers together, we ran all the way from the barn to the house. It felt better than I could describe to feel the wind on my face, the ground beneath my feet - to be here, alive and well, and best of all, to be with Margo.

In her room, we kissed again for what felt like hours. We savored each other, enjoying every moment rather than rushing to the main event. Part of me wondered why we were taking it so slow - we usually had our clothes off by now. But Margo was clearly in charge, and I'd go along with whatever she wanted to do. I already knew it would be amazing.

When I gathered my thoughts, I found myself wondering how getting to this point with her had been so easy. "I thought I had to prove myself to you," I murmured. "I thought I was going to have to do something to make up for lying and betraying you."

"Hm?" She wet her lips, which were swollen and reddened. "You did prove yourself. You showed me you want to stay here."

"And that's enough?"

"That, and what I'm about to do to you." She backed toward her shelf of toys. "Clothes off, my sweet Cherry."

That was the first time she'd called me by that nickname since the accident, and my heart swelled even as my blood ran cold. There was something about that look in her eye - not malicious exactly, but something that said I might not love what was about to happen.

She turned toward the shelf, then looked back at

me. "I said clothes off."

"Yes, Mistress." I stripped down, my heart pounding. "What are you going to do to me?"

Her eyes skimmed down to my waistline. "You've been keeping yourself shaved for me. Good girl."

I flushed. "What are you going to do?" I asked again.

She stepped toward me and pressed me down, onto my knees. "If I don't answer you the first time, that's not an invitation to ask again. Understood?"

I quickly nodded, desperate to show my obedience. "Yes, Mistress."

"Is there a reason that you need to know what I'm going to do to you?" she asked. "Or should you trust that I know your boundaries and your limits, and that you'll like whatever I end up doing?"

A shiver ran down my spine. "Yes, Mistress."

She stroked the side of my face, looking pleased with my humble attitude. She ran her pinky finger over my lips once, then again, until I opened them and let it inside. She slipped another finger inside my mouth while her other hand played with my hair.

What did she want me to do? I wanted - needed - to please her. Looking up at her uncertainly, I wrapped my lips around her fingers and sucked.

Being forced to kneel in front of her had gotten me hot, and as my tongue danced along the length of her finger, my pussy throbbed for more.

How had I ever not known I was submissive? Her dominance turned me on more than anything in the world. When she got strict and stern like this, when she scolded me like a schoolteacher to a child, my desire for her only grew.

Just as my eyes fluttered shut, she extracted her fingers from my mouth with a wet pop. "What a good girl," she purred. "Now get on the bed."

I did as she said, my heartbeat spiking as she brought out the under-bed restraints we'd used before.

"Hold out your arms and legs for me," she said. "I'm going to tie you up the way you like it."

I did as she said, but something didn't make sense. "Shouldn't you be punishing me? Why would you want to do anything the way I like it?"

"Don't worry, my sweet Cherry." The darkness in her voice sent a thrill through my entire nervous system. "You're going to find out."

After securing me tightly, she ran her fingers between my breasts and down to my belly. The sensation sent tingles through my entire body. She was doing the same things she'd done every other time we'd had sex, when she was trying to please me. I couldn't stop myself from enjoying her sensual touches, but I didn't quite trust them, either. Something else was coming, and I had to brace myself for it.

She ran her hands along the swell of each breast, then lightly thumbed each nipple. The expression on her face was normal, even as mine was terrified. Could this be all? Would she really just want to pleasure me? I had my doubts, so I tried not to let myself get caught up in the sensation.

Still, I was a quivering mess by the time she finished toying with my breasts. My pulse was racing, my core pulsating with need. When she stepped away, my fear - and arousal - heightened. Was she going to hurt me? I couldn't see her doing that, she'd always said she was a "loving dominant." But I'd done something that didn't deserve love. What happened now?

She returned from the shelf, her Hitachi Magic Wand in her hands. I licked my lips nervously. I'd looked at the vibrator before, but never tried it. I knew they were originally developed as a muscle massager, and that women had found a different, better use for them. I also knew they were supposed to have some of the most powerful vibrations in existence.

"How would you like me to make you come with this?" Margo asked.

"Very much, Mistress."

Her eyes slid over my peaked nipples and down to my dripping pussy. With my legs spread open like this, every bead of wetness had to be on full display.

She must have decided I was aroused enough, because she placed the toy at my junction. I shuddered when the cool silicone head touched my swollen nub. And that was before she even turned the thing on.

"A-a-a-ah…"

The vibrations were less intense than I'd expected, but I was so worked up that I was sure they'd make me come within about a minute if Margo kept the wand there. My hips pushed upwards as my back arched.

"You're very sensitive," Margo said with interest. "The Hitachi is on the lowest possible setting, and yet you seem like you're almost ready to come." She adjusted the toy slightly between my legs, and the vibrations felt even better. "Is that correct, my sweet Cherry?"

"Yes, Mistress," I gasped out.

"My ripe little Cherry." She took one nipple between her fingers and gently squeezed. "Tell me when you're about to come."

"O-okay." I relaxed into the sensation of the buzzing on my clit. The wand had to be so much more powerful than this. I guessed she'd turn it up when I was about to come. Which happened to be… "Now, Mistress."

She switched the vibrator off.

"Ahh!"

The sound was halfway between a moan and a shriek. My hips thrust upwards, but only met empty air. The disappointment left me gasping, and my arms and legs jerked involuntarily in their restraints. Had that been her plan all along? To build me up to my peak and then not let me reach it?

My eyes met hers, and I quivered under her gaze. She looked so severe, so serious. "Do you know why I did that?" she demanded.

"Because I betrayed you," I shakily said.

"Correct." She grazed the wand over the top of my mound. "And do you know why that was wrong?"

"Because…" I searched for the words she wanted to hear, the ones that would make her make me come. It wasn't hard, since they were the same words I'd been beating myself up with all week. "I broke your trust. I intentionally kept things from you. Important things that you needed to know to keep both of us safe."

She pushed the wand's head over my clit, but without the vibrations, all it did was make me shudder. "And why was that so bad?"

"Because you asked me directly," I panted. "And I lied to your face."

"Mmm." She withdrew the wand, making me

gasp again. "Will you ever do anything like that, ever again?"

That one was easy. "No." The frustration from the failed orgasm still had me trembling. "No, Mistress."

"Do you promise me?"

"Yes. Yes." I would've said anything, I needed to come so badly.

"If there's anything important I should know, you'll offer that information. I won't even have to ask."

"Okay."

"And what will you expect if you ever lie to me again?"

My hips arched up, pushing as far as they could toward that beautiful, terrible instrument of torture.

Margo held it just beyond my reach, looking serious as I struggled to think of the right answer. "What would you expect, Cherry?"

"Break up with me," I finally managed. "Put me on a plane home. Never speak to me again."

Her lips curled up in a satisfied smile. "That sounds about right."

With no warning, she brought the Hitachi back between my thighs. The vibrations hit me at full blast, and in about a millisecond my limbs were spasming against their restraints. I careened over the edge and into a chasm of pure bliss.

I stayed there for what felt like hours, my body rippling as I came over and over. By the time Margo finally took the toy away, I couldn't remember my own name.

She untied my restraints, looking pleased with herself as I fought to collect myself. As she slipped into bed beside me, her arms wrapping around me from behind, there was only one question that remained on my mind.

"Does this mean we're going to keep Harmony as a pet?"

"Yes, Cherry."

TWENTY-ONE

Becoming an official resident of the farm felt as natural as breathing. Margo cleared out some space for me in her room, and I moved my things in. Everything else was the same - aside from the feelings between us.

I loved her, and she loved me. And I was going to stay here - forever. I woke up every day with new purpose. The work we were doing had nothing to do with making rich CEOs richer. We were doing real, manual work - and every time we broke a sweat, it was to put food on our own table.

The summer passed slowly, and we harvested the food we'd planted earlier in the season. I savored every bite of the ultra-fresh, ultra-local food. It tasted so much better than anything I'd ever bought in a grocery store.

My original leaving date passed, and we laughed quietly to each other. The thought of me going back and returning to my old life seemed so foreign as to be bizarre now. Of course I wasn't going to go back to my old job, my old partner… my old miserable existence. Those things were a lifetime ago, and they would stay in the past where they belonged.

My life now was sunshine and fresh grass, dirt

under my nails and hay in my hair. With the love of my life, I was happier than I'd ever imagined.

But not every moment was fantastic.

"Cherry, could you work any faster?"

My back was aching, my legs sore, my arms tired. I put down the shovel to wipe my arm across my forehead. Sweat dripped into my eyes, and I grimaced. "No, I really don't think I can."

"Could you try?" Margo asked. "We're doing this for you, remember?"

I stared at the piles of tires scattered across the front lawn. We were stacking them on top of top of each other and filling each one with dirt. It was back-breaking work that had me dreaming of a nap and a shower.

It was true – I was the one who'd made the comment that the house was a little small for two people. My sister had mentioned wanting to come for a visit, and if she did the place would be really cramped.

Margo had thought about it and said she'd originally built the house for one, never imagining someone else would move in long-term. She decided we should expand the house – tear down a wall and make the living room bigger, adding a third bedroom upstairs. That all sounded great – until I realized that meant we were going to do every single thing ourselves.

"I'm trying," I said. "Can we take a break soon, though?"

"Once we finish this stack."

There were four more tires to fill. That'd probably take forty minutes. I sighed and grabbed the shovel again. My hands were blistering painfully, and even holding the shovel made me wince.

Margo came over to me and took the shovel out of my hands. "Is it that bad?" she asked seriously.

I nodded.

"Then let's take a break." She set the shovel down and took my hands. "My God, look at this. Why haven't you been wearing gloves?"

Oh… that would've been a good idea.

She must've seen the defeat on my face. "Let's get you inside."

In the kitchen, I sat down with relief. She put on the kettle, then swabbed my hands with iodine. I shivered at the contact. Even now that we'd been together for months, her every touch drove me crazy.

"What kind of tea would you like?" she asked.

"Chamomile, please."

She poured a steaming cup for me, then sat down to bandage my hands. Despite the pain, I still enjoyed the contact. I loved how well she took care of me.

"Why didn't you say anything earlier?" she asked when she was finished.

"I thought this was normal." I glanced at my hands. "You were working so hard. I didn't want to be the one to break first."

"I had gloves on, Cherry." She sighed. "And I've done all of this before. Haven't we talked about being open and honest with each other?"

I flashed back to the time she'd tied me up and denied me orgasm until I promised to be open and honest with her. Even after so much time, that still stood out as one of the best orgasms of my life. I'd felt like I died and came back to life. "Yes."

"Yes, who?"

"Yes, Mistress."

The look in her eye made me shiver. Was she thinking our break from work should be a sexy one? I'd definitely be willing – I was ready and eager whenever she said the word – but she was the one who wanted to get the work done, and if we ended up in bed that could easily take hours.

"I think you're done for the day," she said, nodding to my bandaged hands. "You won't be able to use your hands until tomorrow at the earliest."

"I guess I'll have to use something other than my hands," I said, desire rising within me. "Like maybe my tongue."

Two minutes later, we were in the shower upstairs, me on my knees in front of her. I looked up at her worshipfully as hot water poured down on us. I couldn't wait to please her.

She sighed in pleasure as I brushed my tongue across her clit. I kept going lightly for a minute, enjoying her soft panting and the way her fingers laced desperately through my hair. Then I firmed my tongue and went in harder, licking her with the long, bold strokes I knew drove her crazy.

After a little of that, she pushed me away with a groan. "Not yet… want to…"

I smiled to myself. I knew I'd done well when my mistress lost her capacity to speak.

She shut off the shower and grabbed my hand to drag me into our bedroom, pulling a toy from the shelf along the way. We collapsed onto the bed, still dripping wet, and she spread her legs as she handed the toy to me.

I sucked in a breath. She'd chosen a double-ended strap-on, one of our favorites to play with. She liked to wear it with a harness so she could fuck me.

Climbing above her, I pushed one end into her waiting pussy. She moaned, clenching her teeth as it sank inside her. I gave it a few slight thrusts, teasing her, until she gestured at the harness. "Get that on me."

She lifted her hips for me to buckle the straps, and then the toy jutted up from her waistline just like a real cock. But this one was bright purple, and it would never, ever get soft.

"On your knees," she ordered.

"Yes, Mistress."

I knelt on the bed and she sank into me from behind, gripping my ass with a low moan. The toy was a perfect fit, matching every contour of my inner walls - or maybe it just felt like that because of how much Margo turned me on.

My hands twisted in the sheets as she fucked me steadily. The blisters hurt, but right now I barely noticed. The sweet sensations washing over me were so much more powerful.

"What a good girl," Margo cooed, reaching under me to grab handfuls of my breasts. "Who's my good girl?"

"Me."

She circled each nipple with her fingers and squeezed down on both at once. "Louder, my sweet Cherry."

"Me, Mistress." My breath came in gasps. It was hard to speak when she was fucking me like this. "I'm your good girl."

"That's right." She pushed me forward, flattening me on the bed. "And you always will be."

"Yes, Mistress. Yes."

She had me lying on my front now, and there was nothing to do but accept each thrust within my willing passage. I grabbed the mattress, my moans growing louder as her own echoed rhythmically behind me. With every thrust, we cried out as one.

We were so perfect together. I slid a hand under myself so I could stroke my clit as she fucked me. As her speed increased, tension built in my core - a climax beginning to rise. I twisted my head to look back at her and noticed how her beautiful features had contorted in ecstasy. She couldn't be far behind me.

"Mistress," I said, nearly begging. "I'm going to come soon. May I come, please?"

She pressed a hand into my ass and fucked me harder, making my walls contract around the silicone toy. "Not yet. Not until I do."

My spasming was about to go out of control. "Please, Mistress. I can't hold back."

"Just a moment longer." She gripped my rear with both hands and pounded into me, pistoning me with her hips. "I'm not quite there yet."

"But I am. Mistress..."

I tried my best to hold off, not wanting to displease her. I knew she was making me wait so I'd come harder, but God, how could I stop myself? She was slamming into me so hard, each thrust juddering me from the inside. Her hands on me, her scent in my nose – all of it was too much.

My eyes screwed shut, my jaw clenching as I forced back my orgasm. I could do this. For her, I'd do this. But…

"Now," she groaned.

I let go with a scream. My body spasmed, my hips bucking so my clit pushed urgently against my hand. The orgasm washed over me in one giant wave, and as she cried out behind me, a series of smaller waves rocked me into peace.

"Oh my God," I said, trembling as she slowly pulled out of me. "Oh my God."

"You loved that, didn't you?" she asked, sliding a hand over my hip as I turned over weakly.

"I love you, Mistress."

EPILOGUE: FIVE YEARS LATER

MARGO

Cherry had the most adorable smile on her face as she slept. She lay curled up on her side looking like the cat who ate the canary. Maybe she was still dreaming about last night. We'd been up into the wee hours of the night making each other come.

Or maybe her subconscious knew what day it was today.

Five years ago on this date, she'd walked into my life. I'd had no idea it would end up being such a momentous occasion. I thought she'd be like so many of the other volunteers who tried farm life for a week or a month, then quietly decided it wasn't for them.

Back then, I used to ask myself why I bothered to keep accepting volunteers. It took so long to train them to the point that they could help rather than hinder. Often, I thought I'd be better off doing everything alone.

Maybe, the whole time, I was waiting for her.

She rolled onto her back, still fast asleep. Her jaw dropped an inch open, and she let out a quiet snore. My heart filling with love, I gently picked up her hand. As I linked my fingers through hers, her eyes fluttered open.

"I'm sorry," I said. "I didn't mean to wake you up early."

"That's all right. It means I get to spend more time with you."

I bent to press a kiss to her cheek. My Cherry was always so sweet.

"I've been thinking," I told her. "Do you remember when I told you I'd never injure or harm you?"

"How could I ever forget?"

Over our relationship, we'd never done anything that crossed those lines. But… "There's one thing I've been thinking about," I said. "One thing that would make you really mine."

She blinked, wide awake now. "What's that, Mistress?"

"I was thinking it might be nice to put a ring on your…"

She touched her left hand with her right, clearly thinking about the ring I'd put there almost two years ago.

"On your vulva," I finished.

Her eyes went wide, and she sat up beside me. "You mean like a clit piercing?"

"It would be the clit hood, technically. Yes."

"Oh, wow." Her expression went unfocused as she considered the idea. "Would it hurt? And what about sex?"

"From my research, it will hurt quite badly, but only for a second." I stroked her hand. "As for sex, we'll have to wait a little while. But when we do, your sensitivity might be much higher than before."

"Oh-h-h." She liked the sound of that.

"What do you think, my sweet Cherry?" I placed another soft kiss on her cheek. "Would you want to do this for me?"

She looked up at me with darkened eyes. "Only if you'll do the same."

There was no reason to hesitate. If my Cherry wanted me to get pierced for her, then that was what I would do. I was an absolute sucker for this woman. I would've gone to the ends of the earth for her.

I was scared at first, when we started dating. I held her at a distance, terrified of the feelings I was developing. I thought she'd be like all the other city girls. That she'd go back, leaving me alone.

Slowly, I'd realized she wasn't like the others. When she had a chance to go back, she stayed. Although she'd betrayed me, the fact that she came back meant the world. Taking a chance and forgiving her had been the biggest risk of my life... and in the end, it'd been the best risk I'd ever taken.

We drove into town first thing on Saturday

morning – first thing after feeding Harmony, who was still going strong at twelve years old. We'd never gotten another milk goat, so I'd become a little more relaxed about making Cherry do all the work for her. We took care of her equally now, and I had to admit she wasn't so bad as a pet. I'd gotten pretty fond of her, actually. And while I was never going to go vegetarian myself, Cherry's vegan meals weren't bad either.

I'd made an appointment with the piercer over the phone. In person, Liam was a twenty-something with every possible part of his face studded with metal and arms covered in tattoos. At the front desk, he showed us a selection of jewelry we could choose from. "You'll have more options later, but these are good for the initial piercing."

"I like this one for you," I told Cherry, pointing to a simple gold ring.

"I'll get it." She gazed at the tray of jewelry, and then her eyes flashed with glee. "This one is for you." She pointed out a silver barbell with two small cherries dangling from the end.

"Of course." I laughed.

Liam led us into the back room, where he directed me to a bed covered in a white paper sheet like it was a doctor's office. Cherry sat in a chair on the side.

"Now this is something you don't see every day," Liam said as I took off my jeans. "Women your age aren't usually interested in this type of piercing."

I stopped what I was doing, raising both eyebrows. "Oh, really? Will my age interfere with the piercing? Perhaps I should take my business somewhere else."

"Not at all," he quickly said.

He wasn't the first to point out the age difference between me and Cherry, and he wouldn't be the last. I had never cared and never would. Sixteen years younger or not, she was the love of my life.

I lay on the paper sheet and opened my legs. Cherry hurried to my side and took my hand. I closed my eyes as she gripped my fingers tightly.

"Stop that," I told her affectionately. "I swear, you're more nervous than I am."

My smidgen of fear grew as something cool touched my intimate area. I could feel Liam placing the piercing needle between my clitoris and its hood.

"All right, take a deep breath," he said. "In three… two… one."

A flash of sharp pain went through me, but by the time I opened my eyes a second later, it was already gone.

"How was it?" Cherry asked anxiously. "Be real with me."

"It wasn't too bad."

Liam held a mirror in front of me, and I winced as I peered in. Seeing the piercing made it hurt all over again – but the sight of the red cherries on their glittering silver stems made it more than worth it.

Liam gave me a brochure about how to take care of the piercing over the next few weeks. Then, "Your turn," he told Cherry.

I got my pants back on while Cherry took hers off and lay down. As Liam put a new pair of gloves on, I watched the change in her face. She looked more terrified than I'd ever seen her, and I regretted asking her to do this. Maybe this was too much for her – maybe she'd only agreed to make me happy.

"You don't have to do this," I whispered. "You can still back out."

She shook her head bravely. "No, Mistress. I want to."

Liam came to her side, politely ignoring the name she'd just called me – and what it may have given away about our relationship. "Ready?" he asked. "It'll all be over in a second."

"Okay." She screwed her eyes shut. "I'm ready."

I took her hand, and she gripped mine even harder than before. Her gasp when Liam pierced her was full of pain and anguish – but a moment later, she was smiling.

"That's it?" she asked. "It's over?"

"It sure is."

I stepped back to take a look at the gold ring that now graced her beautiful folds. She had a reminder of me permanently fixed inside her body. Even better, she'd be reminded of me every time she touched herself.

The past five years together had been a shock - and a validation. We were made to be together. Our new piercings only proved it.

She was mine. And I was hers.

Forever.

Thank you for reading Mine!

Sign up to my newsletter at http://eepurl.com/dMjIYo to hear about my new releases.

If you loved the book, please tell your friends! You can also leave a review on Amazon or Goodreads.

Turn the page for a look at my other books.

Thank you for supporting an independent author!

Mother of the Bride

When Gloria's daughter announces she's getting married, Gloria couldn't be happier. Things get more complicated when she realizes the groom's mother was her best friend back in high school - the first woman who ever made her heart beat faster, as well as her first kiss. Gloria and Bethany reconnect during the engagement, and Gloria begins to wonder if she could have her own fairytale romance. Is it too late for Gloria to find love? Or could the mother of the bride be the star of her own story?

Scandalous

Lacey is the last person to be impressed by wealth and fame. Serious and stoic, she values hard work above all else. When she's hired as the home care worker to an injured celebrity, she couldn't care less about Zana's carefully constructed image. She only sees a rich, spoiled brat. Once Lacey and Zana learn to respect each other, they actually get along - and maybe more than that. Can Zana win over the one person who sees the real her?

Two Moms

Being a single mom is far from easy, as both Samantha and Joy know. When Samantha's daughter babysits Joy's son, the women are instantly drawn to each other. Each has her own past, but together they have a chance to create something new. Could these two moms end up starting their own family?

Another Mother

Average suburban mom Sarah is suddenly rocketed into the glitzy world of film when her daughter Emma becomes an actress. The strangest part is seeing gorgeous, glamorous Katie Days pretend to be Emma's mother. Sarah is a normal person and Katie is a celebrity, yet they find common ground in the little girl. Could Emma's fake mom become her other mother?

The Marriage Contract

Twelve years ago, Poppy and Leah vowed to get married if they were both single at thirty. After losing touch, the unlikely pair reconnects just in time to meet the deadline. A lot has happened in twelve years... like both of them coming out of the closet. Now the popular girl marrying the science geek is an actual possibility. The contract was only a joke, though - wasn't it?